What people are saying about

Methods Devour Themselves

Taking their cue—and title—from Frantz Fanon, Benjanun Sriduangkaew and J. Moufawad-Paul have refused all methodological straitjackets in this genre-defying book. The result is a chaotically dialectical spiral of fiction-critique-fiction whose form is as speculative as its content, imagining new worlds from amid the crumbling wreckage of the old.

George Ciccariello-Maher, author of *Decolonizing Dialectics* and *Building the Commune*

Compelling science fiction and evocative instant postcolonial criticism entwined in a mutually reproductive double helix. Every page contains an intellectual thrill.

Nick Mamatas, author of *Sensation* and *I Am Providence*

Methods Devour Themselves

A Conversation

Methods Devour Themselves

A Conversation

Benjanun Sriduangkaew

&

J. Moufawad-Paul

Winchester, UK
Washington, USA

First published by Zero Books, 2018
Zero Books is an imprint of John Hunt Publishing Ltd., No. 3 East St., Alresford,
Hampshire SO24 9EE, UK
office1@jhpbooks.net
www.johnhuntpublishing.com
www.zero-books.net

For distributor details and how to order please visit the 'Ordering' section on our website.

Text copyright: Benjanun Sriduangkaew & J. Moufawad-Paul 2017

ISBN: 978 1 78535 826 5
978 1 78535 827 2 (ebook)
Library of Congress Control Number: 2017949638

A CIP catalogue record for this book is available from the British Library.

Design: Stuart Davies

Printed and bound by CPI Group (UK) Ltd, Croydon, CR0 4YY, UK

We operate a distinctive and ethical publishing philosophy in
all areas of our business, from our global network of authors to
production and worldwide distribution.

Contents

To dreamers in the margins and those who came before.

There is a point at which methods devour themselves.
Frantz Fanon

Foreword – Analogical Assemblages

J. Moufawad-Paul

Fiction and nonfiction are only different techniques of storytelling. For reasons that I don't fully understand, fiction dances out of me, and nonfiction is wrenched out by the aching, broken world I wake up to every morning.
Arundhati Roy

In *Science Fiction and Extro-Science Fiction* Quentin Meillassoux makes a distinction between two related subgenres of speculative fiction. According to Meillassoux science fiction (SF) is based on an appeal to a coherent science, whether real or imagined, whereas what he categorizes as extro-science fiction (XSF) violates the rule of theoretical laws. "The guiding question of extro-science fiction is: what should a world be, what should a world resemble, so that it is in principle inaccessible to scientific knowledge, so that it cannot be established as the object of natural science."[1] This genre distinction is less interesting for literary theory than it is for philosophy. Indeed, if Meillassoux was writing an essay that intended to map the genre his claims about the meaning of science fiction—as well as his coining of the imaginary subgenre extro-science fiction—would immediately be undermined. Science fiction is not so easily defined and, once we take into account its long history of sharing genre space with fantasy and horror, the category of extro-science fiction is not as rare in speculative fiction as he seems to believe. The examples of SF and XSF that Meillassoux provides in his extended essay are few and underwhelming. The fact that his analysis is paired with a short story by Isaac Asimov might demonstrate that his awareness of SF is decades out of date and limited to a particular mainstream sample.

But Meillassoux's claims about speculative fiction are not intended to contribute to literary theory or genre history. His seemingly naive claims about literature are meant to function as an analogical argument: Meillassoux's interest is in elaborating a philosophical problem (namely his perspective on Hume's problem of causality/induction) and using what amounts to a *fiction about fiction* to illustrate his position. Hence, while on the surface it appeared as if Meillassoux was making claims about the meaning of literature in this essay, what he was really doing was what philosophers have been doing for a long time with the literature and literary genres they enjoy: mining them for analogical meaning so as to elaborate upon their particular philosophical concerns. The point is not really to explain the meaning of a novel, story, poem, film, or a genre; that is the concern of the literary theorist or the scholar of the history of the arts. Rather, the point is to use this material to elaborate on other concerns that might have nothing to do with the material itself but might be illuminated by analogy.

When we go all the way back to the canonical classics of philosophy we witness this same plundering and slipshod use of the arts. Plato, for example, appropriated Homer and Hesiod to analogically shed light on his arguments despite (and maybe because of) the fact he also despised the ancient poets. Or when we look at the philosophical context from which Meillassoux emerged we cannot help but be impressed by the appropriation of poets such as Mallarmé to illustrate a wild variety of competing philosophical perspectives that Mallarmé himself would not have known or cared to know. (And Meillassoux, following Badiou and others, has also plundered the poems of Mallarmé for his philosophical project.[2])

This book thus takes its cue from Meillassoux's extended essay about science fiction and for two reasons. The first reason is formal: in its pairing with the Asimov short story, *Science Fiction and Extro-Science Fiction* was an interesting publication where a philosophical treatment determined by an analogical appeal to a piece of fiction could share space with the latter so that there was some (but limited) dialogue between the realm of fiction and philosophy. The second reason is provocative: the problematical genre categories Meillassoux established and used to justify his philosophical claims should have indicated to anyone familiar with genre literature that there were a lot of writers and fictions that would challenge his categorization, or at least some who would better demonstrate his claims about XSF. The conjunction of these two reasons is the motivation of this project which is inspired by the following concerns: i) to create an extended dialogue between literature and philosophy with the same analogical motivation; ii) to highlight an author who better demonstrated Meillassoux's category of XSF than the examples he chose; iii) to force the philosopher to engage with fiction that is not an artefact (like the work of Asimov who is dead and cannot respond to Meillassoux's engagement) but in fact the product of a living artist who can also *respond* to philosophical engagement.

When I initially read Meillassoux's essay, and was forced to consider his categorization of XSF, I immediately thought of an author of whom he was unaware. An author who both exemplified and defied his genre categories but whose work I had begun to excavate for similar analogical reasons. This author was Benjanun Sriduangkaew, the contemporary *enfant terrible* of science fiction and fantasy, and this book is the result of my attempt to further engage with her work in a way that Meillassoux was incapable of doing with the corpse of Asimov. It's interesting when a philosopher uses the work of a dead fiction writer to illuminate a philosophical point; it's possibly more compelling if this writer is still alive, can respond in kind, and extend the analogical dialogue.

3

Sriduangkaew's organic speculative fiction at the conjuncture

Benjanun Sriduangkaew's work emerged at a particular speculative fiction conjuncture: when the genre was gaining more literary credibility, when some of its non-white and non-Western authors were being nominated for awards (and she received such nominations), but when various fan communities were invested in protecting the supposed boundaries of the genre. The pushing of the boundaries and the subject positions of some authors involved in this pushing resulted in a predictable backlash from fans, rhizomatically unified across various social media sites, who wanted their favourite books to be taken seriously but to also remain unchallenged. The attacks on women of colour genre authors who received critical acclaim in the form of nominations and awards, the "gaming" of the Hugo awards by right wing trolls, the snide dismissal of "sensitivity readers" in the name of free speech, and the disdain for literary quality in the name of genre purity are all characteristics of this conjuncture.

I do not wish to explore this conjuncture in too much detail because it would take us beyond the bounds of this project. But if Sriduangkaew's work emerges from this context then we should understand the general meaning of this emergence. Therefore, it is necessary to point out this conjuncture's main contradiction since this book was conceived in a space produced by this contradiction's problematic. On the one hand we are presented with authors, a significant portion of whom come from marginalized communities, producing new concepts— sometimes with literary acumen—and thus mobilizing for change and development. On the other hand, there are authors and fans who, despite their complaints that science fiction and fantasy fiction is not being taken seriously by critics, resist all critical engagement. Whereas the former category might succeed in demarginalizing speculative fiction by bringing it into contact with literary theory and academic analysis, the latter category

4

seeks to keep the genre pure and free from the contamination of change, what might result from literary engagement and debate, despite (ironically) its long-standing complaints about stigmatization.

What I find particularly interesting about the above antinomy is that some of the significant authors devoted to challenging and thus demarginalizing speculative fiction from the genre cantonment are also authors who occupy sites of marginalization: people of colour, queer, trans, differently-abled, and voices from the global south. Subjects at the peripheries of global power are publishing perspectives that are crystallizing into new permutations of genre fiction. Conversely, those who seek to keep speculative fiction marginalized generally benefit from, or are at least complicit in, the dominant structures of social power; because of an interest in preserving the state of affairs they believe that their beloved genre should be accepted by everyone without critical intervention.

In such a context Sriduangkaew's fictional output was significant, even becoming notorious, for the following reasons: i) it cut across the boundaries of science fiction, fantasy, and horror in a manner similar to "new weird" authors such as China Mieville, thus reinforcing the idea that speculative fiction could be transgressive and wildly imaginative; ii) it evinced a concern for the abstract philosophical ideas that has always made speculative fiction a literature of concepts; iii) it was driven by a progressive political ethos that liberals working within the genre and broader SFF community would find too radical; iv) its form and style was intended to be literary rather than "popular".

When one reads a story or novella by Sriduangkaew one cannot help but be struck by a richness and depth that is held together by an impressive command of syntactic and semantic formal structure. Sofia Samatar and Catherynne Valente are other contemporary speculative fiction authors who match Sriduangkaew's literary skill. Although Valente is also a master of philosophical concepts, genre violations, and transgressive gestures, only Samatar is Sriduangkaew's peer on the level of political radicalism. And yet Sriduangkaew, unlike Samatar, is the kind of political writer that has been notoriously invested in "the ruthless criticism of all that exists."

Therefore, as a political philosopher interested in speculative fiction for its imaginative potential, I find authors such as Sriduangkaew extremely interesting. Because of its richness, I have already used her work as an analogical device for my own philosophy on more than one occasion. Elsewhere I have referred to the deep "organic" nature of her literary production in the sense described by Gramsci: "millions and millions of social infusoria building up the red coral reefs which one day in the not too distant future will burst forth above the waves and still them, and lull the oceanic tempest, and establish a new balance between the currents and climes. But this influx is organic, it grows from the circulation of ideas, from the maintenance of an intact apparatus."[3] This quote describes Sriduangkaew's work and the reason it demands philosophical engagement: the "circulation of ideas" that has resulted in a literary "oceanic tempest", the latter of which has grown from a coherent literary apparatus. Such an organic literary irruption is precisely what a philosopher finds interesting. Sriduangkaew's work, in its organic depth, is primed for analogical appropriation.

As noted above Sriduangkaew is one of the authors who came to mind when I read Meillassoux's concept of XSF. Of course, Sriduangkaew is more than capable of writing fiction that remains within the boundaries of SF. For example, her story *The Universe as Vast as Our Longing*—one of her most heart-shatteringly poignant tales—unfolds within a traditional space opera setting but, eschewing the dominant imperial narratives of this trope, demonstrates a commitment to an anti-colonial ethos. *Parable of the Cocoon* is another example of Sriduangkaew's ability to remain within SF boundaries, though demonstrating how far these boundaries can be pushed without becoming insensible to scientific knowledge, as she writes about alien visitation and theories of parallax time. Much of her work, when it is not what is classified as Fantasy or Magic Realism, is precisely what we could call XSF and I have often wondered how Meillassoux would have written about this category if he was familiar with Sriduangkaew. Indeed, those stories that take place in her fictional universe of the Costeya Hegemony are space operas concerned with a reality that defies modern scientific sense: characters who have become living beehives, exhale prophetic petals, live incarcerated with thousands of versions of their self. Or the grim story of *Comet's Call* where a living comet mercenary is hired to solve the riddle of a machine that is murdering an entire civilization through ancestral lines, a machine that defies all scientific reasoning and can only be thwarted when it is not treated as an "object of natural science."[4] The list could go on.

More interestingly, though, some of Sriduangkaew's work demonstrates how Meillassoux's category of XSF loses its coherence when faced with literature that breaks traditional SF boundaries. For example, in the story we chose to begin this collaboration, *We Are All Wasteland On the Inside,* we are met with a "Zone" type event[5] where our reality has collided with the reality principles of a mythic order so that all the rules of physics are at first "rendered inaccessible to modern science." As readers will notice this inaccessibility is formalized in the prose and descriptions of a world colonized by phantasmagoria; the opening description of a plague/curse victim is mind-boggling, forcing the reader to think around causality. And yet, as a defence mechanism, scientific knowledge is re-established since the poetic and artistic imagination have been rendered null by a reality structured around unbounded fantasy: the only way to remain sane and to survive is to resort to empirical wagers and positivist tools.

Thus, to return to Meillassoux's formula of XSF, while it is the case that "the question of science is present in the tale, albeit in a negative mode," it is not the case that it is "always excluded because of the frequency of aberrant events."[6] In fact it is more accurate to say that the science in this story "subsists without subsisting as a whole," and though this might in fact imply "that [science] has completely collapsed in its general coherence," the only reason it "continues to haunt the universe" is precisely because its form has been weirdly retained.[7]

This project is not guided by the desire to elaborate Meillassoux's thoughts on the genre. Highlighting the ways in which Sriduangkaew's work intersects with Meillassoux's conceptualization demonstrates the level of depth that the former possesses and how this depth might be elaborated by the latter's analysis of the genre. While I'm sympathetic with stories that might be called "XSF" because they are ripe for philosophical engagement, my interest in Sriduangkaew is also, as aforementioned, motivated by my interest in a commitment to a liberatory politics particularly at this genre conjuncture. The fictional openings she indicates, the ways in which her stories can be used to illuminate revolutionary arguments, the cultural counter-hegemony of which she is a part demands engagement. I am thus interested in the dialogue that results from a prolonged engagement with her work: what subjectivities it will encourage, and the possible meaning of this dialogue when the author also replies through fiction to a political philosopher who has drawn from her work.

Engagements

The essay engagements with Sriduangkaew's fictions should not be treated as reviews or even critical analyses. They are not intended to be works of literary theory let alone claim to unlock some "inner truth" of the fictions with which they engage. Rather, they are motivated by the desire to mine deep fictional troves for analogical ore. Sometimes when we read a story we are reminded of concerns and problematics that were not part of the author's intentions when she crafted her fiction. Stories also reflect the interests of the reader who might be able to force and develop a unique sense of meaning retroactively through a critical reading. A reader can take elements from a story and use them to think through ideas that may have not crossed the author's mind: multiple analogical moments are encountered in a single reading; passages and characters signal an isometric engagement.

When philosophers with particular concerns read a story or novel, especially if such fictions are burgeoning with potential meaning, they often find their concerns reflected in the narrative— that is, they encounter potential analogies for their own thought. Such encounters, I would argue, emanate from work that possesses the kind of organic richness that, as noted above, is inherent to the work of authors such as Sriduangkaew. Indeed, as noted above, there is a reason why multiple French thinkers have used Mallarmé as an analogical prop for their philosophy; why Benjamin kept returning to Kafka; why Adorno obsessed over Proust; why Fanon drew upon Depestre and Fodeba; why Mao in his most philosophical moments conjured the fictions of Lu. These were all works that, due to their complexity of both form and content, implicated critical engagement.

Of course it might indeed be the case that thinkers can find analogical encounters in thoughtless and petty works of literature. Take, for example, Zizek's obsession with jokes and mundane Hollywood movies. I would argue, however, that the result of such pithy encounters are either ironic or banal— much like their source material. The analogical claims derived from such engagements are usually predictable or at best not very interesting.[8] But let's not get bogged down in literary theory and claims about artistic quality. Better to recognize that some literary geographies are more lush than others, based on an appeal to philosophical intervention as a whole, than to get sidetracked by a discussion of the meaning of aesthetic quality that is beyond the scope of this project.

Just as philosophers and theorists have drawn from fiction and poetry to elaborate their concerns, so too have fiction writers and poets drawn from philosophy and theory. We only need to think of the immense influence of Marxism and then post-structuralism/post-colonialism upon the arts to realize the truth of this relationship, or the ways in which Aimé Césaire and Frantz Fanon have influenced large swathes of anti-colonial literature. Moreover, long-standing debates over particular philosophical problems—identity, time, mind, causality, language, scepticism—have often been translated into plot devices in popular speculative fiction.

Philosophy and theory have inspired fiction just as much as fiction has inspired philosophy and theory; there is a mobius circuit running between these different modes of communication. Large swathes of fiction, from the avant-garde to mainstream genre, would not be possible without the ideas and concepts originating from philosophy and theory. Try to imagine Ngũgĩ's *Devil on the Cross* without Fanon. Or, to cite a pop culture example, try to imagine the Wachowski sisters' *Matrix Trilogy* without Descartes. Authors like playing with ideas; fiction would be pretty boring if they did not.

While I am not suggesting that I'm the kind of thinker worthy of fictional engagement, in my responses I will be drawing upon those who are and, in the process, highlighting concepts and problematics that hopefully coincide with Sriduangkaew's own interests. Her work to date is already marked by engagements with radical political philosophy; it will not be difficult for her to bypass whatever awkwardness I might bring to the discussion and focus upon areas that already form part of her creative concern.

Three fictions and three non-fictions form the following assemblage that—beginning with the initial story and read in order—represents a kind of conversation or dialogue. The aim of this experiment is to produce something approaching a dialogical whole: the essays developed out of an engagement with the stories, elicited by some idea or concept, a turn of phrase or an analogy burgeoning with philosophical possibility, but are distinct entities. Similarly, the stories following the essays originate from something in these essays that provoked a fictional response. Although we start with a work that was previously published, because it initiates the conversation, everything following this foundation is the dialogue.

Hopefully this conversation will contribute to the conjuncture of speculative fiction I discussed above, declaring fidelity to the position that pushes the boundaries and resists backlash. The collaborative nature of this project—and the ways in which our methods devour each other so as to eke out a liminal space that is both and neither story and essay—might permit interrogations and contestations that cut across our respective ways of knowing. If speculative fiction has always been a constellation of genres that intersect with philosophical concerns, by making these concerns explicit we can reinforce resistance to the genre counter-revolution that seeks to conserve and prolong all of the conceits and retrograde gestures of an uncritical fandom. The aim is to use this dialogue to aid in the development of a new genre fandom composed of reader-militants who will think of speculative fiction as part of a larger counter-hegemony. Speculative fiction can and should be linked to the ruthless criticism of the contemporary and brutal state of affairs.

Chapter One

We Are All Wasteland On the Inside[1]

Benjanun Sriduangkaew

She is dying, the old spymaster, when I visit her house. Spread all over the room: lethargic on the bed, a hand (thick, callused) pinned to the ceiling, a leg (long, shapely) dangling from a bookshelf. The rate of her decay has been rapid, toxins mating and making nations in her body, fighting wars and creating cultures and making history that expresses in the bioluminescence blotting her skin. It looks editorial, opal tones and swallowed sea-storms, and would have made her the star of a body-mod exhibit. Jellyfish chic, arising salt-thick and hungry from the deep.

But still she breathes and when she sees me, she says, "Help yourself."

The bar is fully stocked, red bottles and faceted cups. Clean stirrers, cleaner glassware. She has a housekeeper, some fresh-faced (as they eternally are) upsorn-sriha newly out of the forest: the sandals left at the door are telltale, delicate gold and shaped for hooves. For my drink I pick smoky wine and red petals that dissolve in the alcohol, giving up spice and salt and sour. I skip the coconut syrup that's supposed to go with the cocktail. Sweet things are not my province.

I settle on a chaise lounge. It's distracting, her collapse, the slow agony of a body pushing free of each other as though they are similarly polarized magnets. Phantom limbs have sprung from the sockets of her arm and leg. They curl about her, boneless, barely real in their pallor. Her torso is intact otherwise, the head still firmly joined to the rest. A pre-murder scene, avant-garde and carefully posed on sheets and headboard for maximum statement. She must be on anaesthetics, medulla oblongata sloshing in drugs, but her eyes are steady, her voice smooth and uninterrupted by intoxication.

"I'm your assigned legal executor." A sip: as hard-hitting as I expected. She has good taste and the means to satisfy it, though I can't imagine she has enjoyed anything lately. "We'll need your authorization to unseal your will, Khun Jutamat."

Her mouth pinches. A smile aborted late-term. "I don't have one."

That's news to me. I know she has close family and two ex-wives. "Your property will revert to the state."

"I'll be dead and money won't matter to me. I didn't ask for you specifically on account of your law degree. You worked with police."

"Yes, ma'am." I have worked in many things: theatre, accounting, a stint in forensics and vice. Mine is a timeline in disarray, but so are most people's. Much of life has become debris and dead skin after Himmapan, the convergence event.

Jutamat's poltergeist arm stretches unsteadily, the movements more like limp rubber than bone and muscle. Undulating, repulsive. "It's a good range of skills. Much more important than one's bank balance or where that balance goes after one expires. You and I, we'll solve my murder together before I go."

In Jutamat's garden there is a tree, old, its canopies dripping star-shaped leaves. Gold, green, tipped in stark white. It is heavy with a crop of makkalee fruits on the cusp of maturity and independence from the bough. I have never seen one of these trees; they don't grow just anywhere and resist attempts at cultivation. Only at the liminal edges do they flourish, where Himmapan hovers and seeps into city, black loam making sludge of asphalt, green radiance splattering traffic signs and sidewalks. Where birds fly too close to that border they disappear, the dirt-crusted pigeons and smoke-stained crows.

Accordingly there are no birds here or butterflies, no ants or amphibians. All is clean. Not a blade of grass is too long; no weeds or infestation of fungi touch the earth, no mark of worm or insect hunger on petals. Frangipani, lotuses—either Jutamat favours those, or no other flower would grow. Symbols of passing on and peace, respectively. Appropriate perhaps.

Myth tells that makkalee fruits are alluring and sweetly scented. Reality is less glamorous. They smell faintly vegetal rather than like palm sugar, jasmines, or some heavenly blossom. On the ground one of them lies fallen and premature, ivory skin bruised from impact and seeping blue sap. I turn it in my palm, tracing the contours of full breasts and small waist, flared hips and thick thighs. The face is rough, a work in progress, but there is already a nose and mouth defined, eye sockets deepening. The ones on the bough are shaped similarly. All makkalee fruits from the same tree look alike, replicated over and over in some internal mould, the way dolls emerge from a factory.

"Have you ever met one of them full grown?"

I put the fruit down. Jutamat's wheelchair labours, for all that her mass can't weigh that much anymore. Shreds of her ghost leg get stuck in mechanism, between joints. "Can't say I have, ma'am."

"Poor conversationalists. They only think of the soil and the air, rain and sun. Not much else; I can't imagine what hermits in legends see. But then, mythical hermits tend to be ugly and desperate." She wheels forward. It continues to be a struggle, looking at her directly. The eye protests. Optic nerves flinch. The mind attempts to reconstitute what is there and fails. "Rumour has it that eating makkalee will cure any ill. Incorrect, of course. My housekeeper planted this, by the way, to keep her company— not many Himmapan natives live in the neighbourhood. Would you like a bite? Think of it like moulded chocolate or marzipan."

"I will pass, thank you." I don't consider myself squeamish. But still they look humanlike and, given time to ripen, they will talk like humans too. Pastiche personhood. "I don't think I am the person you want for this." A simple arrangement of paperwork, what will go where, a list of beneficiaries and then a cut for the tax collectors. That is what it should have been.

"I'll be the judge of that. You were police, more or less."

"Less rather than more." With effort I focus on the banal details: her thinning hair, the indented scar on her chin. "What makes you think there's a crime to figure out, a perpetrator to bring to justice?"

"Justice has nothing to do with it, Khun Oraphin. I seek satisfaction and, from your records with forensics, you seem to have a nose for the strange. When you were very young, you were lost in Himmapan for a day, I understand."

A day to my parents; a month to me. It wasn't a bad month— Himmapan is kind to children, and I was twelve going on thirteen, sufficiently young and sufficiently pure—but I returned changed, one of the first to have made the crossing before true convergence. No one believed me, at first, until the parents of another child went on air. Talk shows, taken seriously by nobody, and then a handful of lost children grew to a dozen, a score. We became a generation. Himmapan, the domain of many things, but foremost among them the eagle and the serpent. When I open my hand I half-expect to be clutching a feather the colour of clear night, the colour of polished cobalt. This is a hallucination that's seated itself deep inside me, parasitic, cancerous.

"I suppose I was, ma'am." I never say anything else. Not the details. Not anything.

"Stop calling me that. You aren't my servant." Her flesh leg twitches; she is trying to cross it, but the other one is insubstantial and does not obey. I wonder if the amputated leg, alone in that room, flexes and pulls with effort. "I was one of the people poring over your case file, back then. It all looked like a threat to national security at the time."

Sixteen years ago. "What'd you like me to do, Khun Jutamat?"

15

"Help me figure this out," she says. "My fortune isn't going anywhere. It's not inconsiderable—you would know. It would serve a dead woman poorly, but you're alive and prone to stay that way for decades yet. Sort this out and I'll sign it all to you."

Her assets are significant, no denying that. My thoughts dart—avarice is so magnetic—to the possibilities, the fantasies, the horizons out of reach. Money is not all, especially in the changed world, but it is still much. Humanity does not function without a currency. We've knotted ourselves too tight to go back to barter and an exchange of labour, to discard the coins and the notes and the cheques. Even those of the forest are becoming like us in that way. "Your family isn't going to be happy with me."

She issues a low chuckle, a sound of paper rustling on wood. "What does it matter, whether they are happy? Come, I'm not dying any slower. The sooner we get started, the better."

To trace any curse, the most obvious and essential first step is to examine the site of its effect, in this case Jutamat's body parts. There will be a piece of buffalo hide, a fragment of tooth or finger-bone, as vector for malice. I imagine the housekeeper on her dainty deer hooves dusting the celadon and polishing the teak floor, precise steps as she cleans around these lost limbs. Not everyone can afford upsorn-sriha staff, hard workers as well as supreme ornaments. All the rage in any establishment of class and currency, any household of taste and opulence. For myself I can't stand those quiet hooved girls, but I am no tastemaker.

With gloves on—best practice must be followed—I pull down the detached limbs. The hand is first and hardest, speared in place by a reptilian tongue of glistening iron. It bleeds when I bring it down, though Jutamat evinces no reaction save mild amusement. The leg—it is a whole leg, complete, from thigh to tiptoes. Fetching it is simple; handling it less so. The weight of the limb is hot and heavy, confrontational in its gross mortality, the bones and muscles and wrinkled skin at the knees. I seize it around the ankle at first, then reverse my grip when I realize that the position would put the thigh much too close to my face. Manoeuvring it awkwardly to a sofa I put it down and try not to think on the intimacy of this. The detachment happened right at the point where it joined the groin, clean.

The leg smells faintly of shower cream, not the cheap type: this is essential oils, bergamot and frankincense, an underlying note of subtle fruits. The poison must have preserved the parts entirely, suspended them in the moment of amputation. "What were you doing when this happened?"

"I'd just come out of a bath. That was the first one." Her voice falters, only just, then resumes smooth: lifetime-practised control sanding off the edge of trauma. "How does it end?"

"Your head." Not that I have seen it in action but there are reports and studies. Few ailments of supernatural sources have not been catalogued, compared, cross-referenced into mundanity. We forge the changed earth through empiricism and remorseless analysis. The poets and dreamers thought they would be ascendant, but after all it's people like me and Jutamat who thrive. Pragmatists who know how to move through the world, and know how to move it in turn by levers and hand-wheels. "It's mostly painless. As far as I know, ma'am."

Jutamat makes a noise through her teeth, strained and thin and high: distilled panic. "Two to five months, though they say it escalates toward the final stage."

"Do you have enemies?"

"In my profession, at my age, who does not? Unless one is devoted to nothing but pushing pens and shuffling papers. Any number of people, domestic and foreign, would want me gone." She sips from a glass of anchan tea so cold it radiates, mentholated and lambent. "After sixty I'd have thought they would leave me alone to die naturally. I guess not. Should've smoked and drunk more."

The past doesn't relent and deeds like hers don't fade, not

that she needs reminding. When I open her detached hand it feels exhibitionist—perhaps voyeuristic?—to be caressing, touching, playing with an older stranger's appendage. Her palm is empty: I'd expected a sliver, a thorn, the swell of a small tooth hiding under skin. The obvious carrier of a curse. If only, for once, existence would oblige by being simple. "Have you been having dreams?" Sleep paralysis, a ghostly face greenly lit. The paranormal is predictable in its symptoms, easier than viruses and cancer to diagnose, more straightforward by far than the caprices of human flesh.

"No dreams. No, that's not quite true. One dream. A khrut. Young. Female. Four arms. She's sitting on a chair. Blue like her feathers." Her expression pinches: this is not a woman used to sharing her dreams. "She's singing, I suppose, but there is no sound. Like you are receiving faulty signal, visual without auditory."

I look at the leg, perfunctory, pushing at the skin and peering behind the knee. "I will need to consult."

"Who, a shaman?"

"No." The leg falls from my hand and rests, limp, on the table. It will leave smudges on the glass and the housekeeper will have to wipe that away. She will have to put the limbs somewhere, too, arrange them in neat order. Maybe a mannequin, custom-made to Jutamat's build. "I will get back to you as soon as possible."

Throughout all this, she has not asked how to stop the toxin of unmaking. Some curses are like the common flu. Others are cousin to genetic defects, unliftable, incurable. It sits there inside, cystic slag hardening to fossil, a seismic fault-line in the soul. The only answer is passage into the next life.

Reincarnation is the true panacea.

There's nothing magical about Krungthep. The writers and artists were wrong, and what once resided within their fantasias and imagination are now everyday—everywhere. Metaphor and allegory no longer serve, having turned literal overnight. Even the statues and stencils in Suvarnaphum have come alive, adopted as vessels for the creatures they once depicted as fictional. What is the point of words on pages, or nielloware etchings or delicate carved ivory, when the genuine articles are full of voice and viscera?

It's strange: others who have wandered into Himmapan as children, the ones I know, none of them turned to art when they grew up. Not painting or sculpting, not the piano or the jakhe, neither verse nor prose. Those from the forest make better images and music than we do in any case. Maybe we are *meant* for brute industry and surgical calculation while they are built for the rest, including philosophy.

Every time need summons me to Suvarnaphum, I bring vast quantities of food. They trend red, a menu selected for the carnivore's palate. The giants can eat fruits and vegetables like anyone else, but they enjoy those no more than a child, and unlike a child they don't need to worry about cavities, caloric intake, diabetic futures. Himmapan beings can eat as much as they like, gobbling up carcinogens and cholesterol with no cost or effect.

The giants make their home where first-class passengers used to check into Thai Airways, under a pavilion of banana leaves that never brown. Few travellers venture near for fear of the giants' appetite, and not without reason. There have been disappearances, though never remains. There have been questions, though never investigations. I do know for a fact that the giants are tremendous eaters and that they leave no bones.

All three are home today, reclining on cushions made from hammered bronze and holding plates made from black nacre. Empty. Around them, the walls gleam with tableaus of holiness. Prince Siddhartha stepping on the lotuses of his birth; Prince Siddhartha forsaking his palace to seek the ascetic's path; Prince Siddhartha triumphing over demonic temptation.

As one the giants look at me, or at least turn their attention. Each of them has four faces apiece with eyes to match, their gazes reading existence in compound. Their faces are theatrical masks, red and blue and green, bristling tusks like machetes. Wood and acrylic transmuted to sinew and iron. I've asked them why they don't wear their own flesh and get answers in verse that leave me no more enlightened. They have an abiding love of Sanskrit, which I never bothered learning (does anyone, who was once spirited away?); that is the province of a government liaison (I avoid that entire division—too many fetishists).

"Child," one of them says, "you did not come empty-handed; we can smell."

This is a ritual—they don't talk without a bribe. The Styrofoam boxes I brought are damp with blood and grease: cartilage flavoured hot and sour, dripping meat just barely rare, plastic jars of namprik and dry chili. Pork, beef, the animal is nearly moot. As long as it is flesh that once belonged to a walking creature, flesh that once housed cardiac muscles the size of a fist. I don't think much of vegetarianism, but if anything could turn me herbivorous it would be them, not religion or even health problems.

Once they have filled their plates, the blue one says, "You look in want of a tale."

The green one chuckles, a sound like a landslide about to begin. "We tell stories not to excite or intrigue, but to harden their truth."

(*Don't you have names?* I asked. *The crunch of femur and the slide of tongue on new guts,* they said. I didn't ask again. You could call them Morrakot, Tuptim, and Pailin, but those are such soft names next to their predator might.)

"I don't. I need to know—" My breath trembles, cuts short, a juddering knock against my teeth. "I need to know if Panthajinda is alive."

They look at one another. Enough eyes to spare, still, to look at me too. "You left a wound in Himmapan, child." This from the red one, though they all have the same voice, asphalt and seismic calculus. "It seeks to restore itself, in khrut-shape or not."

I was a child, I could say; I did not know what I was doing. But the actual meat of it, the reality, is what it is and will not bend to my excuses. "Let me talk to her." What remains of her.

The green giant opens their mouth, and keeps opening. Past the unhinging of jaw it opens, a gaping hole lined with bright tongues and red teeth. I have seen it before, and don't look away, but it's not a sight I wish on anyone. The tongues and teeth roar and blur into a vermillion haze. Himmapan colours bleed into that with difficulty. Sometimes I don't think the giants are from the forest at all; it is a place of green and gold and opal radiance while the giants are red on red inside, a hungry insatiable mass.

The image stabilizes and there is Panthajinda, enthroned, eyes shut. When I left her and Himmapan, we were both children, but her echo—spirit remnant, dregs at cup's end—has aged, tall and strong, her four arms immaculate. Two for the wings, two for human things. Droplets of water in her black-sun hair, on her gilded throat. She looks asleep; of course she looks asleep, a goddess at rest.

How do you begin to apologize, even if it wasn't your fault? How do you start to grieve, when you are as good as the murderer? The giants don't judge or condemn, but they don't have to.

We don't talk; what communication occurs is at a preverbal level, the sensation of elevating pulse and heart knotting into stone, the memory of dying. Wisdom passes from her to me in impressionistic blots, truths on mortality and samsara that turn like barbed wheels. The dead don't have secrets to keep. They tell you everything, everything. All you need to do is ask, all you need to have is the stomach to bear.

I promised myself I wouldn't cry; it leaves me small and brittle, robbed of dignity. I break this promise, every time.

21

On the train ride home I watch a girl, seventeen maybe, compulsively blotting her face. Sheet after sheet; she is too sweaty and the air conditioning too sluggish. At the far end of the carriage, two kinnaree murmur in quiet conversation, fair salaries and weather, the merits of birdseed and imported fruits. Their foreheads and noses produce no excess sebum. Their eyelashes are voluminous without the requirement of mascara, their lips pink without the assistance of lipstick, their skin lustrous and poreless without the help of foundation. Enough of them and the cosmetics industry will go extinct entirely. Himmapan women make farang supermodels look pickled and haggard, farang celebrities overpainted and swollen with Botox.

Back at my apartment, I take out the lockbox that has accompanied me from move to move down the years, home to dormitory to apartment. It's small and mundane, a dial lock to guard it and not much else. Few pieces of jewellery are attached to my name and all of them reside here, but the star is this: two bangles beaten thread-thin, clinched together by a star sapphire. The one gift from Panthajinda that she intended to be the first of many. Funny really; it was given to a child, but somehow it's stretched as my wrist grew, the gold so soft and so warm. I rarely wear it. For two days I don't leave my apartment, pulling blackout curtains over the windows, double-bolting my door, switching off my phone. An anechoic chamber, liberated from human interaction.

On the third day, I return to Khun Jutamat's house, the bangles gleaming on my wrist. I'm dehydrated, famished, and my head is full of feathers.

She isn't home, but one of her staff lets me in on her instruction. Wait in the garden, they say; she'll be back shortly from the hospital. Perhaps some miracle cure has been found, last-minute. Most likely not.

Her garden overlooks the Chao Praya, which isn't what it used to be, that mucky sewage-blighted self. After Himmapan and Krungthep collided the river has been running clear, its skin lacerated nacreous white, smelling of cleanness and payanak and—toward the sea—mermaids. To filth the waters is to court incredible misfortune, swifter and harsher than falling apart slowly. So much converges, so much moves inexorably. What Himmapan brought is not magic but consequence. What happens to us, inside, is a wasteland.

The upsorn-sriha housekeeper steps, dainty, onto the veranda. The tray she carries holds a perspiring glass. Her eyes are downcast, demure. You always forget the damage an upsorn-sriha can do, they all have this look of harmless grace, their delicate feet made for running. Away, you think, because of the folktales. Kinnaree, upsorn-sriha, makkalee fruits, all the girlish things of the forest who exist to be captured, painted, admired.

I take the glass, gazing into it, the milky tea. It's flat, bright orange, the same colour a child might shade in a sun. I think of drinking it in one big gulp, emptying the glass just like that and grinding the ice to dust in my mouth. "Is this painful?"

"Pardon, ma'am?" Even her voice is ordinary. Her face too, plain and homely as though she's been particularly cursed among a species made for breathtaking beauty.

"Whatever you added to the tea. Will it put me to sleep without pain, or do you mean for me to suffer like Khun Jutamat did? Or worse."

Her gaze meets mine, direct, before fixing on the bangle. The star sapphire that is so like the colour of Panthajinda's wings. "She was meant to be a queen among khrut."

"I remember you now." A handmaiden, or childhood companion. Panthajinda didn't give her much attention during the time I was in Himmapan; I was novel while the upsorn-sriha was not. She used to hover just out of sight, dutiful and a little sad, I thought. "You must've been there when she died."

"She wouldn't have been there near the river, had you not

slipped. So close to the territory of her enemies. They were at war; still are."

It's not as though I need reminding. The war between nak and khrut, that forever enmity between those of the water and the sky. Serpent against eagle. As a child I didn't understand it; as a child I thought only of Himmapan as a vast playground, freer than any Krungthep street. "I couldn't have known." That the nak would drag her in and drown her; that her wings—strong on land, impossibly mighty in flight—would be deadweight in water, no use at all. "She was a child."

"She would have grown to rule and command. They destroyed her as they would any weapon. I will avenge her, but their logic wasn't unsound."

The nak spared me, once my purpose as bait was past. Because I was a human child, they said, and to take a mortal life was a sin. Not so with another of Himmapan kind. With others of the forest, any tactic was permissible, any death a justification unto itself. "Would this even bring her back?" Killing Jutamat, killing me.

She stares at me, unblinking. Do deer need to blink, I wonder. "It's not the flesh—Khun Jutamat, like you, is mortal—but the essence, the karmic heft. Some are bound for better destinies than others. You should pay for what you did, but your place on the wheel is far beneath what I require. Khun Jutamat is gold. You are dross."

How strange that the spymaster is, evidently, possessed of greater virtue than most. Than me, though that's no surprise. "What is still there..." My breath comes out thin. "It's not her anymore."

The first hint of anger: "What do you know about my liege."

Nothing, nothing at all. An image, a memory. The dead bear no resemblance, a distant cousin to their living selves. Less. "How many more do you need?" Counting cargo, reducing it to simple arithmetic.

"If I find a single shining soul, rich and pure, it will suffice to give her a new body. I will need nothing more."

"Isn't this prohibited for you." Human lives: Jutamat's and whoever else's, before and after. How many in total, I could ask, balancing a chequebook. Murders against one resurrection, crimes against one act of reparation.

Her hands twitch; her shoulders coil, tense. "I may be exiled. But I will see her back."

Isn't that what love is like, after all. What I feel for—about—Panthajinda is tangled in an ideal. I slide the bangles off my wrist, hold them out to the upsorn-sriha whose name I have not asked (and would she tell me? No). "Take it. More yours than mine."

She might move to slap it out of my hands, out of pride. Instead she takes those thin gold threads and puts them onto her wrist. Slimmer than mine, and already the bangles appear to fit as though they'd been made just for her. She doesn't offer, *But she would have wanted you to keep them.* No quarter.

When she's gone, I drink the tea. Not too sweet, not too much condensed milk. It's just right and it's just tea, unburdened by the acrimonious acid of poison or curse.

When she was still alive, I asked Panthajinda what Himmapan would have been like untouched by human imagination; how the wars would have played out, how each race would have evolved, deific and alien. *Meeting you is the best thing that ever happened to me, Oraphin,* she said. *I can't wait to see your Krungthep, all your skyscrapers, all your lights. We could go to school together.* After she died, I asked her again, and it was then I learned that the dead do not use words, do not speak. Instead she showed me an image, a dark line stretching forever, drinking all light: an event horizon, full of ruin, the endpoint of Himmapan crossing over. There is no room for dreamers.

On the way out I take a final look at Jutamat's lost, forlorn limbs, stacked together in the living room. Two legs, one arm.

Soon she will be simply a human torso, and then not even that. Maybe that is the future. An epidemic of disassembly and all of us lying exposed, apart, awaiting the end.

I will be there too. By then Panthajinda will have come back, picking a path through the vision she foresaw. She will glide on her taloned feet, the upsorn-sriha at her side, and stop by my body. For one last time, I will see her again.

Chapter Two

Debris and Dead Skin: the capitalist imaginary and the atrophy of thought

J. Moufawad-Paul

Fukuyama's thesis that history has climaxed with liberal capitalism may have been widely derided, but it is accepted, even assumed, at the level of the cultural unconscious.
Mark Fisher

We are nearly two decades into the 21st century and occupy a world cluttered with objects and phenomena that would have been scarcely imaginable even in the middle of the 20th century. All of the dreams of the fantasists of the 1950s are eclipsed by the reality of technological development; the science fictions of the 1960s are largely outdated. And yet we have also failed to transcend the limits of even 19th century imagination: despite all these new technologies, many of which must appear like magic to our long dead counterparts, the world is still determined by the logic of capital. Whereas a 19th century utopian imagined a future that transcended exploitative and oppressive social relations we are losing our ability to think outside the capitalist box. Following the so-called "end of history" our imagination has atrophied. Is it any wonder, then, that much of the world still resembles the hell on earth reviled by past socialist thinkers? As dystopia becomes normative everywhere—endless wars, increased exploitation in the global peripheries, a resurgence of fascist movements in the imperialist metropoles, environmental devastation—it is much more difficult to imagine a time beyond these centuries of capitalist logic.

Our imagination is becoming thoroughly capitalist.

The victory of the capitalist camp secured this dystopian monopoly on imagination. Since cold war ideology had already succeeded in valorizing a dystopian literature where all resistance to capitalism and imperialism was coded as "totalitarian" and doomed to failure (Orwell's *1984* and all of its imitations), its greater success was in passing off its own dystopia as reality itself. Hence, the most powerful capitalist nations would loudly proclaim that they possessed moral credibility—and these proclamations were accepted as "common sense" by their citizens—and were free and open societies while they subjected the majority of the globe to harsher regimes of exploitation and oppression. Eighty per cent of the world was transformed into a massive concentration camp, all resistance to neo-colonialism was brutally crushed, but since none of this resembled the totalitarian dystopias the capitalist camp had ascribed to their defeated cold war enemy, history was over and we were stuck with "the best of the worst" which was also called *democracy*.

By the time the crisis of 2008 erupted the end of history discourse and the institutional maintenance of this discourse was so complete that imperial subjects, certain they lived in the freest countries on the planet, were collectively unable to recognize that things were even worse than the Great Depression. At the same time there was also an explosion of new dystopian literature, though most of it was written for Young Adults, as if to signify that people were aware that reality had become dystopian. Unfortunately, if such an awareness existed it was mainly unconscious; the vast majority of this new dystopian literature (*The Hunger Games*, *Divergent*, etc.) was just a rehashing of tired tropes about "totalitarianism"; the authors seemed unaware that the world in which they wrote was far more dystopian than their plagiarized fantasies from *Battle Royale*, *1984*, or *Brave New World*. A world in which a bunch of people have to fight in an arena to secure social peace is in fact less nightmarish than a world in which an entire country can be slated for re-management, as

Haiti was in 2005 by US Americans and Canadians at a summit to which not a single Haitian was invited.

We are living in a world that is more dystopian than dystopian literature and this fact generates two popular responses: ignorant denial or cynical acceptance. Both of these responses are determined by the capitalist purchase on thought since, having conceived of itself as the end of history, part of capitalism's dystopic power is in its ability to prevent thinking from transcending its limits.

Capitalism as the normative order of existence

Benjanun Sriduangkaew's *We Are All Wasteland On the Inside* describes a world in which the reality of the mythic Himmapan forest has collided with our own. The former laws of space and time are degraded, subjected to a new totality sutured from the alterities of Himmapan and modern Krungthep (Bangkok). A state of horror becomes the state of affairs for the denizens of both formerly separate realities. Hungry giants with four faces— whose names are "the crunch of femur and the slide of tongue on new guts"—occupy airports; existence "has become debris and dead skin."

Instead of treating this story as just another iteration of "Zone" literature (such as *Roadside Picnic*, *Nova Swing*, or *The Southern Reach Trilogy*), which in many ways it is, I find it more useful as a metaphor for the colonization of imagination affected by the capitalist end of history. For the detective story Sriduangkaew tells unfolds in a fictional landscape where the Himmapan event is so total that it assimilates imagination itself:

The writers and artists were wrong, and what once resided within their fantasias and imagination are now everyday— everywhere. Metaphor and allegory no longer serve, having turned literal overnight. Even the statues and stencils in Suvarnaphum have come alive, adopted as vessels for the creatures they once depicted as fictional. What is the point of words on pages, or nielloware etchings or delicate carved ivory, when the genuine articles are full of voice and viscera.

Once the fancies of the poets and myth-makers insinuate themselves in the everyday they necessarily subject our creative faculties to a regime harsher than any totalitarian institution of censorship; the realm of fantasy, which is also the realm of desire, is censored by reality itself. What kind of literature would exist in such a world? A kind of realism, based on a reality where the beings of fantasy have become banal, that will become more monotonous than the social realist moral tales we imagine were commonplace in past socialist regimes. The story's protagonist in fact laments that the reality of a tree that grows living beings is "less glamorous" than the myth that proceeded convergence.

I would like to suggest that this story's mythic dystopia is in fact the world in which we live; we are indeed living in a time where the fancies of the poets and myth-makers of yesteryear are commonplace. While there are no ogres or living trees, the technological development in the past two decades has resulted in a reality that would appear phantasmagoric to a time traveller from the 1950s. And yet this fabulous world of smartphones, tablets, 3D printers, self-driving cars, etc. remains limited *by the boundaries of capitalism*. In a telling passage Sriduangkaew writes:

> Few ailments... have not been catalogued, compared, cross-referenced into mundanity. We forge the changed earth through empiricism and remorseless analysis. The poets and dreamers thought they would be ascendant, but after all it's people like me and Jutamat who thrive. Pragmatists who know how to move... it in turn by levers and hand-wheels.

All transformations unimaginable a generation earlier remain dominated by capitalist techniques of positivism, the rule of the bourgeois technocrat. Despite even the most unanticipated and fantabulous transformations, reality is recaptured by capitalist one-dimensionality. If we could impose a moral to such a fantastic story it would be thus: no matter the transformation, and regardless of what some "accelerationists" might think, while it is possible to imagine and accept the strangest transformations of our fundamental existence, the barriers of imagining how to end capitalism, let alone how to think outside of capitalism, remain daunting. Our fantasies are not only totalized and rendered banal, they are subordinated to the normative order of existence.

Capitalist realism and its purchase on imagination

The late Mark Fisher used the term "capitalist realism" to describe our inability to think beyond the capitalist imaginary. Capitalist realism, according to Fisher, is "the widespread sense that not only is capitalism the only viable political economic system, but also that it is now impossible even to *imagine* a coherent alternative."[1] Before Fisher numerous left thinkers had already analysed the end of history discourse that had taken on a life beyond Fukuyama's initial pronouncement. Despite the fact that the maxim "history is written by the winners" is an eye-roll inducing cliché it has not really been applied to the history of the cold war as written by the capitalist victors that declared themselves history's consummation. Perhaps there is a compelling truth contained in this cliché. The fact that there is a general unwillingness to critically engage with the discursive historical claims of the victors of the cold war by the very same people who mindlessly repeat this saying about the writing of history demonstrates that it not only holds some truth but also defies the thought of those responsible for its promulgation. That someone can claim that "history is written by the winners" while simultaneously accepting the narrative of the cold war victors is telling: it demonstrates the strength of capitalist realism, the omnipotence of the capitalist imaginary, and the "end of history" discourse's monopoly on reality.

We can also use Marcuse's concept of "one-dimensionality" to describe the ways in which capitalism draws boundaries around thinking, socializing us into accepting that there can be nothing of value beyond the limits of the bourgeois order. Generally, and especially in the imperialist metropoles, we are meant to believe (and this belief is very compelling) that the way in which capitalist ideology describes reality—its imaginary—corresponds with reality itself.

Obviously the anti-capitalist left has rejected the ideology of capitalist realism for as long as the latter has existed; if it had not done so it would die a quick death. One cannot be an anti-capitalist, after all, while consciously agreeing that there is no point in struggling against capitalism. What I'm suggesting, however, is that despite our critical rejection of the diktat of the capitalist imaginary it has still influenced the way in which we engage with reality. The result is an atrophy of thought. Such a suggestion should not be controversial for those who believe that social being influences social consciousness: having grown up in a capitalist social formation we have been socialized according to its categories; resisting its hegemony is a lifelong struggle. Former leftists who "grow up" and become liberals, or worse conservatives, are just individuals who lost this struggle, for whatever reason, and were yanked back into a proscribed framework of reality. What might be controversial about my suggestion, however, is in how I see the affect of capitalist realism upon the left, particularly since I think this atrophy in thought persists even within critiques of this phenomenon.

Indeed, the strongest boundary the capitalist imaginary enforces is between the "end of history" present and our understanding of past communist catastrophe. The reason why this boundary is significant is because a discourse that describes communism as out-and-out failure reinforces the claim that a communist future is always doomed. The result is a left that is haunted by its past, and most of the left in North America might agree that this is the case. But usually the meaning placed on this haunting is precisely the meaning determined by the capitalist imaginary: we are haunted by the failures, by all the mistakes our forebears have made. I am not suggesting that our communist past was not filled with mistakes (if it was not then the entire history of the cold war would be different), but I hold that this wallowing in tragedy is the kind of thinking encouraged by capitalist ideology, particularly the ideology reinforced by cold war dogma. Jodi Dean refers to this wallowing as a melancholia where "the Left is bent around the force of loss, that is, the contorted shape it has found itself in as it has forfeited or betrayed the communist ideal."[2]

The strength of the past to linger as a ghost lies in its ability to disarticulate any meaningful analysis that can inform our practical struggles. We see only the failures of revolution and are usually conditioned to ignore the successes. We often refuse to grasp the precise nature of world historical revolutionary successes—hard won by the sacrifices of the oppressed—just as we refuse to grasp the *whys* and *hows* of the parallel revolutionary failures. The justification for this claim is that, since the declaration of "the end of history", the anti-capitalist left at the centres of global capitalism has unilaterally failed to produce a coherent and combative movement. It has not seized victory from the proverbial jaws of defeat and part of this is because of its inability, as a whole, to produce a concrete assessment of the conjuncture. We are at a point where fascism is re-emerging, as we should have known it would, and we do not yet possess the kind of fighting organization or united front that is disciplined enough to respond to this challenge.

Thus, there is a strong and knee-jerk reaction even amongst Marxists to the suggestion that, in order to get beyond the movementist malaise, we need a "new return" to the conception of the fighting party that is derived from a critical assessment of the two great world historical communist revolutions of Russia and China.[3] Despite the fact that when I have made this claim in the past I have also critically qualified it by stating that such a return must not be a revival of a "Marxism-Leninism of an old type", my suggestion that there were great successes we need to learn from, and that we need to find ways to grasp the failures that are not determined by cold war ideology, immediately meets a limit in thought. The common response is: it was all a failure, we need to think of new methods of organization and strategy, to even consider value in past patterns is the sin of orthodoxy.

On the surface such a response, motivated by a supposed heterodox appeal to new methods, seems to be an endorsement of the kind of creative thinking forbidden by the capitalist imaginary. Its apparent strength is that its critique of programmatic party politics is intended to be a declaration of a practice that pushes beyond old patterns of thinking. The truth, however, is that this supposedly imaginative way of thinking beyond the limits of capitalist realism is, like the poets and artists in Sriduangkaew's story, conditioned by the "debris and dead skin" of atrophied thought. What is in fact truly forbidden, and what is declared outside the logic of the capitalist order, is not the pursuit of vague and supposedly "new" ways of organizing. Rather, what is anathema to the capitalist imaginary is a style of thinking and work that excavates our revolutionary history, and the lessons learned from this history, that can teach us something about the weaknesses of this reality.

The limits of thought

The militant at the centres of world capitalism is in fact forbidden from imagining that the communist sequences of the past can teach us something about the limits of capitalist reality. In this context, the fetishism of novelty is widespread. This search for the new holy grail of anti-capitalist theory is akin to a poet in the fictional universe of Sriduangkaew's story attempting to develop a new style of art in a world that has rendered the fine arts largely meaningless. Capitalist realism is not challenged by the supposedly new characteristics of social movementism because it has always been able to absorb these characteristics. What is far more bothersome for bourgeois hegemony, and that produces an imaginary that exists in defiance of the one demarcated by capitalism, are unified movements that seek to be comprehensive, fighting, and revolutionary parties.

We only need to look at the struggles outside of the imperialist metropoles to realize that it is not the novelty of social movementism—of inchoate social movements with no direction beyond the spirit of rebellion—that grips militants pursuing long-term anti-capitalist/anti-imperialist projects. The sequence of people's wars since the early 1990s to the present tell us a different story. These were programmatic and disciplined movements that based their organization and strategy on lessons critically extracted from the past. Despite the fact that many of these movements failed—in Peru, Turkey, Nepal—they were still making revolution, and sometimes even coming quite close to victory, in a context where so-called radical intellectuals and respectable leftists, whose thought was claimed by the capitalist imaginary, were arguing that such movements could not even exist.

And yet the strength of capitalist realism is such that it encourages a very particular way of engaging with social movements in the global peripheries. Therefore, right at the height of the people's war in Nepal—a movement that, before it was claimed by the old revisionist patterns of practice, was producing new conceptions of organization and strategy, and new articulations of theory—the first world left was more interested in the Egyptian movement of the squares. Despite the fact that this movement was incoherent, and was easily claimed by reactionary forces and then a military coup that reinstalled the old regime, because it looked like first world movementism it was accorded more interest than a far more radical people's war. It is thus difficult for militants in the imperialist centres to look to the global peripheries for direction because their ability to even perceive these peripheries is immediately filtered through a capitalist imaginary: they can only see what they are already proscribed to see.

If we look at India and its current people's war the struggle between atrophied left thought and a revolutionary movement that rejects this impoverishment is acutely apparent. The Communist Party of India (Marxist) is an official government institution that participates in the repression of Naxal insurgency; meanwhile the greatest security threat to India and the imperialist interests in India is this very insurgency, led by the Communist Party of India (Maoist), who are classified as "terrorists" by the CPI(Marxist) because they won't get with the programme of capitalist realism or, more accurately, comprador-capitalist realism. India thus demonstrates a clash between an "end of history" type of thinking and a radical imaginary that rejects capitalist realism within the left itself. This clash sharpens when CPI(Marxist) intellectual ideologues deliver talks at academic conferences about the need for "creative solutions" to the problem of making revolution only to walk off the stage when supporters of Naxal insurgents demand that they explain why their party is not opposed to the suppression of an active people's war that is precisely the "creative solution" they seemed to be describing.[4]

Hence, while it is indeed the case that a rejection of capitalist realism is prevalent in the peripheries, it is also the case that leftists in the imperialist centres do not want, as a whole, to recognize this rejection because it does not accord to the patterns of behaviour they have inherited from end of history thinking. When ideologues of comprador "left" organizations endorse this way of thinking this atrophy in thought is justified. A people's war that is still the number one security threat in a peripheralized nation can be ignored, despite the fact that the most powerful capitalist countries are spending billions in military aid to put it down, and first world leftists can instead focus their attention on inchoate uprisings that look precisely like the novel ways they have conceived of their own struggles. A warped pragmatism reigns supreme, just as it does in Sriduangkaew's Himmapan event: if we accept that the capitalist imaginary is normative, and that all fantasies to the contrary are rendered banal, then it is simply a matter of damage control. The dreamers behind a people's war, masses of revolutionaries who reject this logic, might as well not even exist.

Beyond "Stalinism"

Of course we *do* need to think new methods of organization and strategy. But if we are critical of the ways in which struggle has been conceived by this first world inspired capitalist imaginary, I think I'm quite justified in claiming that the organizational and strategic concepts that are often passed as "new" are in fact quite old even if they have been rebranded. Movementism is just a modern iteration of an age-old anarchism; left refoundationalism is what the anti-capitalist left has been trying to do for decades. And when it comes to the concept of strategy—when it is not being conflated with organizational structure—we've mainly been treated to different forms of the same insurrectionist substance that was considered normative since 1917. Indeed, the problematic of strategy is paradigmatic of an impoverished imagination.

At the end of the 1990s the now defunct Quebecois organization Action Socialiste declared despairingly: "The fact is that 150 years of Marxism—including all its vitality, its energy, its intelligence and resources—should have been oriented in an almost singular direction: solving the question of proletarian revolution." They lamented that the left had not solved this question because it had instead accepted the theory of insurrection: protracted legal struggle, general strike, a beautiful moment where the proletariat arms itself, a rapid civil war that splits the forces of the state. Hence, despite all of the talk about new theoretical developments, despite all of the novel conceptions of organization, it is quite telling that the normative strategic conception—so normative that it is rarely examined in a critical manner—is one inherited from 1917.[5] In the midst of demands for creativity there is a stark lack of creativity in the one area that should matter: making revolution. This lack should not be surprising since an imagination conditioned by capitalism will necessarily find it difficult to think the one thing this imagination holds as truly monstrous: the annihilation of capitalist reality.

Leaving aside the question of strategy, which is its own difficult problematic, lurking behind this knee-jerk rejection of my suggestion of a "new return" to past revolutionary sequences is a conception of reality conditioned by the capitalist imaginary. What is really going on is that any appeal to the past that wants to treat its successes as precedents—even if it is qualified that such precedents must also be developed out of an assessment of failure—is dismissed according to a vast machinery of anti-communist ideology established by the cold war and sanctified by the "end of history". Liberals have a name for the communist threat: *totalitarianism*, one of the worst concepts produced by Western thought, a discourse primarily designed to associate communism with fascism. First world leftists have their own name, which pretty much means the same thing: *Stalinism*. While I am not arguing that we should return to Stalin's conception of Marxism-Leninism, I do believe that one of the ways we are kept from critically engaging with our past is due to this concept-that-is-not-a-concept called Stalinism, unfortunately reinforced by the fact that adherents to Trotsky's political line have been more active in Western intellectual circles for the past three or four decades. The reason I think Stalinism is useless as a concept, and why it forbids critical historical memory, is because it lacks historical and theoretical coherence: when the Soviet Union under Khrushchev, Brezhnev, and then Gorbachev and Yeltsin are all called "Stalinism" then there's an obvious contradiction inherent in the concept.[6]

Hence, even those who recognize the way in which capitalism delimits thought have a difficult time thinking beyond these limits. In *Capitalist Realism*, for example, Fisher in fact uses the term Stalinism to describe the ways in which contemporary capitalism manages market exchange.[7] But Stalinism is a pseudo-concept produced by capitalist ideology so as to reinforce what Fisher calls "capitalist realism" and thus linking the former to the latter should be treated as strange but, because of the strength of capitalist realism, is not judged as such. We should all be familiar with the liberal cliché that communism is "good in theory and bad in practice", a mindless truism that enforces the capitalist imaginary. A core doxa of this truism, though, is that any attempt to transcend capitalism will end up resembling this vague Stalinism where "some pigs are more equal than others", a centralized market will reduce everything to a repressive and drab collectivity, and terrible iron-fisted catastrophe will become the norm.

The capitalist imaginary replaces the truth of the "socialism or barbarism" antinomy with this groundless maxim: "capitalism or Stalinism". Although Fisher's entire work on capitalist realism was dedicated, and masterfully so, to demanding a return to the recognition of the former antinomy, he unintentionally valorizes the latter. By conflating contemporary capitalism with Stalinism he places socialism beyond the horizon of our atrophied thought. If all real world attempts to make socialism are branded with the charge of Stalinism—and contemporary capitalism is even worse, according to Fisher, because of its "market Stalinism"— then what else exists that can launch our atrophied thought beyond the boundaries of the capitalist imaginary? Only

Trotskyism or some form of anarchism, one would assume, but this is entirely convenient since these are traditions without a significant revolutionary legacy. Such a discourse forbids us from engaging meaningfully with anti-capitalist history.

Moreover, in using the signifier of Stalinism in such a manner, Fisher appears to be implying that capitalism is worse than it would be otherwise because of this qualification: contemporary capitalism is worse than classical capitalism because of a characteristic derived from *communist* history. Capitalist realism thus seems, if we are to focus only on this interpretation (which we should not), to be derived from a cold war hatred of socialist realism.

We are so thoroughly haunted by the poltergeist of capitalism that it becomes difficult to comprehend this haunting except by its own terms. Reaction to Trump's election in the US is a perfect example of how decades of anti-communist ideology has produced a common sense inability to reject capitalism's most senile manifestations. Faced with a crisis in the liberal order—an order that had erroneously conceived itself as the opposite of fascism—US mainstream resistance to Trump's election could only conceive of the latter in terms of what the former had been conditioned by capitalist realism into thinking was the greatest evil: communism. Thus Trump, despite being an extreme but logical symptom of capitalism, could not be seen as such since capitalism was understood as the end of history. The great evil of communist "Stalinism" has been mobilized to critique Trump's regime because, after decades of cold war propaganda and a pitiless hatred of socialism, what could be worse than communism? Newspaper cartoons with hammers and sickles have become common; conspiracy theories about Russian tampering with elections, despite the fact that Russia has been capitalist *because* of the end of history, and diatribes about Trump's "Stalinism" are everywhere.

Since fascists are quite aware that communists are their

natural enemies, and have done their damnedest to confuse the masses (i.e. the Nazi terminology of "National Socialism" was mainly coined to pull would-be socialist workers into a national capitalist project), Bannon gleefully encouraged this misunderstanding by ironically referring to himself as a "Leninist". Liberal ideologues, who love to take fascists at their word, broadcasted this disinformation. Capitalist realism reigns supreme: it is indeed easier to imagine the world according to capitalist categories, even when these categories have become non-sensical, than dare to think their transcendence.

Behind the barriers in thought

The barrier in thought we encounter when apprehending the past isn't limited to the more distant events of previous world historical revolutions; it also has to do with movements closer in time. Take, for example, the New Communist Movement which represented a period of massive organizational agitation against capitalism throughout the world. Motivated by the Cultural Revolution in China, anti-revisionist communist organizations proliferated on every continent; in the global metropoles these kinds of organizations diverged from the so-called New Left of early 1960s radicalism. Despite the fact that the New Communist Movement greatly eclipsed the New Left in terms of numbers and organizational discipline there is very little assessment of this period.[8] Since it met its limits at the end of the 1980s following the victory of the "capitalist roaders" in China and the dissolution of the Eastern Bloc its significance was undermined by the consummation of the capitalist imaginary at the altar of the end of history.

Due to its attempt to declare fidelity to a critical and anti-revisionist Marxism-Leninism, the New Communist Movement was drowned by the tide of victorious capitalist ideology and thus relegated to a limbo that resisted investigation. It was as if, despite all the literature and accounts that claimed otherwise, this period of struggle had never existed. In the imperialist metropoles, where the capitalist imaginary is the strongest, we are fed a particular narrative about 1960s radicalism: hippy peaceniks, an incoherent New Left, a milquetoast interpretation of the Black Panthers, and then a "growing up" that is best represented by Reagan and Thatcher.

What we must not recall, though, is that the moment when capitalism declared its end of history is also the moment when revolutionaries declared a new stage of revolutionary science: the People's War in Peru. Such a declaration and the sequences it unleashed with the Revolutionary Internationalist Movement, revolutions in Nepal and then India, must also not be thought. After all, such recollection defies what is acceptable for an imagination conditioned by capitalism to think beyond its limits in the very moment it declares itself eternal. All histories outside of the singular history of capitalist victory are forbidden: when they are not condemned to amnesia they are interpreted as naive or totalitarian mistakes.

My contention, which should not be controversial, is that we should engage with these kinds of histories and refuse to forget the sacrifices or dismiss them as museum relics; the time in which they operated is not entirely alien to our own. We need to refuse the total denial of our past and learn the lessons forbidden by an imagination disciplined by capitalism.

Capitalism abides

So what, then, is the solution? Due to the problematic I have described—the capitalist imaginary, capitalist realism, the end of history discourse, etc.—it becomes quite difficult, by definition, to answer such a question. Radical theory has in fact provided justification for this difficulty. According to Althusser the creative subject is nothing more than the interpellated product of ideological state apparatuses, a completely socialized fabrication; Foucault and other post-structuralists went further by suggesting a complete decentring of a subject that could think outside of oppression, a subject that could only reinscribe the totalization of reality in even its revolutionary attempts. The protagonist in Sriduangkaew's story is symptomatic of this difficulty: despite being a detective hired to solve the problem of a curse, she is also a child who was stolen by Himmapan in the early days of convergence, discovered her subjecthood in a tragic romance that produced her sense of self, and thus cannot think outside of its reality; the entire mystery is compromised by the fact that she is part of the very problem she seeks to solve.[9] In such a context, then, to even conceive of a solution to the capitalist imaginary is itself met with a barrier in thought that results in three apparent problems.

First of all, if thought is thoroughly atrophied then we cannot answer this question or even properly conceptualize it; such a total understanding undermines critique itself, rendering everything I've said contradictory. Secondly, and as I'm suggesting, if the way to answer this question is to recapture the lessons from the past, resist historical amnesia, and concretely connect with revolutionary sequences in a manner that rejects capitalist realism, then we encounter some serious difficulties, much like the difficulties encountered by the protagonist of Sriduangkaew's short story (a detective attempting to force meaning, based on her understanding of an eclipsed and obscured past, upon the mystery of her dystopia), because we have been forbidden from thinking this past. Thirdly, due to the problems I have described, the mention of even the slightest opening to a solution culled from a sequence of past revolutionary time is also classified as forbidden, exiled by an imagination disciplined by capitalist ideology.

These three problems can be unified in an unflinching apprehension of the imagination produced by capitalist realism. Such an imagination insists that it persists beyond the limits of physics itself; it would claim purchase upon a reality that is even torn asunder by an event like Himmapan's infection of Krungthep in Sriduangkaew's story. The phenomena of sheer fantasy can walk the streets, the rules of space-time are threatened, and yet the capitalist imaginary is convinced that it will persist.

Capitalism abides in thought, even when we argue for its destruction, colonizing all of our attempts to conceive its destruction. It is the "debris and dead skin" of thought that chokes our imagination as its economic and political processes smother existence itself. It will permit its own hungry giants waiting in ruined airports just so long as these forces of violence can be "move[d]… in turn by [its] levers and hand-wheels." That is, by the laws of the market which, always conceived like Smith's invisible hand, are just as mythic as ogres and magical forests. Capitalism has always loved the mythic order just so long as this order can be subordinated to its logic: the story of Odysseus, as Adorno and Horkheimer discussed, becomes a tale of bourgeois cunning; Jesus justifies private property; a "work ethic" is located in the New Testament; a variety of new mythologies, like the self-made man and the cult of the individual, proliferate. In many ways capitalism *is* the mythic order of Himmapan that has collided with human existence, subordinating reality to its brutal imaginary.

The reality of this imaginary, however, is one of immanent catastrophe. As I have argued elsewhere, following Rosa Luxemburg and the revolutionary tradition, if the limits of this reality are not transgressed and the logic of capitalism is allowed to persist then the world will be thoroughly devastated, our material grounds for existence annihilated, and this vicious system will devour us along with itself. "Maybe that is the future," Sriduangkaew writes: "An epidemic of disassembly and all of us lying exposed, apart, awaiting the end." In a very real sense, and according to the systemic logic obscured by the capitalist imaginary, this is indeed the future.

The only way out is to rupture from this imaginary and its

purchase on reality. Hence, the philosophical project to which I am devoted, and which I have written three books about so far, concerns the (re)discovery of a coherent revolutionary past beneath the closures enacted by the capitalist imaginary, this history's unfolding according to historical necessity, and the ways in which such a past can be logically conceived so as to breathe life into the present.

Chapter Three

Krungthep is an Onomatopoeia

Benjanun Sriduangkaew

On the shipworld's skin they find her half-dead, pierced by the shrapnel of her chassis and seared by the spill of her fuel. They have to saw through cables and melt through blueshift alloy, unravel the latticework of couplings and wirings that connect flesh to processor, and even in her catatonia she cries out in pain at each separation.

They do not dare to part her from the pilot's cradle, so fused is she to the seat and the frame: her nerves to sensors, her muscles to controls, her tendons to bulkhead. Instead they carry her entire into the shipworld, part human and part machine and barely alive, the wreck of her beautiful even in this moment close to the end. The lustre of satin-glass that grows out of her scalp in place of hair, the geometric perfection of her silhouette, the jagged prisms of her dream that transmits even now into the whorls of the shipworld's cortex. She is the sum and total of human accomplishment.

While they lay her down on her deathbed, the cortex sorts through her dreams, which have pushed forth in reflex like blood gushing from a wound.

First: the pilot is clasped in her cradle, one with bulkhead and trajectory, a star through the dark. She is not alone. There are three of them together, knitted by complex decisions and compromises and something the cortex understands as affection.

Second: the pilot is on her knees and one of her companions is a mass of rot and gangrene, his body failing him, the augmentations of his limbs and liver in rapid decay. He reeks of mortality. There are two of them left.

Third: the pilot is cradling a gun and she is firing it, a single shot—this close, she cannot miss—into her last companion. The bullet cuts a clean, painless path through skin and skull and the death is immediate. This dream replays, over and over. Grip on gun. Trigger pulling. The bullet clearing the chamber, and then the pilot is alone.

When queried, the cortex says, "Her dreams do not contain the answer you seek. Her dreams do not contain her duty and service, the directive to which the shipworld's destiny may be yoked. Her dreams do not say whether humanity can go home."

They query the cortex as to how this crucial answer may be obtained.

To which it says, "As for that, only the pilot can tell you."

The shipworld is called Krungthep after the city in which it was built. It has been made to last: the central matrix-column takes the shape of a banyan tree, its vermillion canopy housing the cortex that calculates, regulates, and sustains the three hundred thousand that inhabit Krungthep's decks.

Suranut has seen the original Krungthep in records and knows that the shipworld is nothing like it: no canals run between the decks and partitions, fluorescent with lantern-eels. There are no ferries that glide close to form market islets and bridges, no ropes of golden prayers billowing in the sky at visakha bucha. There *is* no sky.

A sky suggests possibility, opens up infinity, cannot be measured. A sky is vaster than the shipworld which is enormous but has precise limits: Suranut knows its dimensions by heart, like any child born to the decks. These thoughts have consumed her since an age she could comprehend what *sky* meant, what its presence in the old media of Earth entails, what its absence in the shipworld declares. Its absence, the shape of *no* and *cannot*.

When the cortex summons her, it is the sky that she is dreaming of.

She is authenticated into an elevator she's never seen before, the carriage opaque with combinatorial poetry. When she steps in and touches the inner wall, the verses leap and rearrange around her fingerprints, coiling around her knuckles and thumbs. One of them bites—a pinprick, surgically precise—and then the cortex's voice blossoms in her ear.

"Esteemed citizen," it says, between alto and tenor, in the formal register. "You have been selected on strength of your likely affinity toward the subject. Along with two other candidates, you will be assigned a trial period to interact with the subject, to test her responsiveness to you and vice versa."

In her thirty-eight years this is the first time Suranut has heard the shipworld's voice.

"What is this about?" she asks, expecting no answer and is given none. No doubt the intention is for her to enter the situation unbiased. The cortex didn't even send an official to soften the summons.

Under the glow of serpentine verses, she looks at her fingertip where the cortex injected her with receptors. Bloodless; she can barely discern the puncture-point. Suranut wonders whether this is a permanent change, whether she would always be able to hear the shipworld.

She meets the other candidates in a chamber lit by the cortex-cloud. One is an older supply-accountant in his sixties, the other a teenage girl no older than seventeen. As Suranut opens her mouth to greet and introduce herself, the cortex murmurs in her ear, "Esteemed citizen, it is requested that the candidates do not converse either during or after the trial period. This is to ensure the purity of result."

Biting down on her lip, she finds a corner and sits, her hands clasped on her stomach. One by one they are called, disappearing into different doors. They must exit elsewhere, for by the time Suranut's turn comes she still hasn't seen either the girl or the accountant. Or perhaps the cortex has deemed them lacking and directed them to the recycling plants—but this isn't a thought she entertains for more than a moment. The shipworld terminates residents humanely at the expected end of their lifespan.

Her door is a trapezoid. The passage behind it stretches long and subterranean before her. Distant noises she recognizes as owl hoots; she's seen the birds in the zoo, those beaked somnambulists. A second ambience runs in counterpoint, more strident. Reference index lets her know they are audio files of cicadas, randomized into organic play. Where her feet fall she feels not the hard tiles of shipworld ground but something that bends and rustles.

She emerges into a chamber shaped like a bowl.

In the centre, the *subject* in a vast bed. Tethered to the ceiling by life support, each cable as thin as puppet string. Tendrils of satin-glass frame her face and disappear into the loose gown that gives her modesty. Her ankles flare, khrut-like, into taloned metal feet.

Suranut gasps, too loud, before she can stop herself.

They've all heard of this. Begun decades ago as a classified project, to build a vessel to reconnoitre humanity's shattered home. The craft itself was, and is, trivial; finding a crew who could survive the journey, conscious the entire time and sane, was a greater challenge. How many were selected and sent forth remains secret.

And here is one. Perhaps the only, or—

"The last one." The subject's eyes are still human, or mostly so. Pinpoints of light in her irises spin in slow circles. "You're the last of them, aren't you?"

Suranut draws a breath. One step and she pauses, unsure whether she's meant to approach.

The cortex again: "Please address the subject as Pilot."

Abruptly she makes a decision. Forward, until half a metre separates her and the bed. "What do I call you?"

The pilot draws up her legs, a slow considered motion. Talons scrape along without tearing the mattress. Perhaps the cortex is whispering in her ear, instructing her not to answer or to answer with her function rather than her name. But she says, "Gullaya. My name's Gullaya."

Suranut's fingertip flares with sudden, intense pain. She understands the warning well before the cortex speaks.

"Esteemed citizen." The voice stays perfectly neutral, not that she expects any different. "You may leave."

The second summons is an ambush: Suranut did not expect to hear any more of it, see any more of the catacomb-chamber or the pilot Gullaya.

She is woken up at twenty-three thirty, two hours after she's finished work and gone to sleep. No hand on her shoulder to shake her into consciousness, but she wakes nevertheless and in the dark comes face to face with a cloud of red fireflies. The shape of it approximates a person at the foot of her bed, the mouth full of flame-teeth like forever candlewicks.

"Khun Suranut Tanawiwat." The torso bows; the hands make a shapeless wai, insect-form fingers blurring into one another. "Your presence and grace are requested in the healing-house of Pilot."

"She has a name." Bedsheet pools at her waist. Suranut doesn't bother to cover herself; there is no privacy from the AI, from birth to termination. "Why?"

"You ask more questions than average, esteemed citizen. You are requested."

"She has a name," Suranut repeats.

"As does the body that houses the AI, citizen, but few would refer to it or the collection of processes and algorithms that form the cortex as *Krungthep*."

For a moment she stares at the shifting haze, not real but substantial in spite of that; it does not dimple her mattress or char her duvet, but she can't escape the impression that if she reaches out she will touch a corporeal presence. Will be, perhaps, singed. "Are you offended? That we don't use your name. It's not as though most of us ever get to speak to you."

The avatar's head cants. Astonishingly humanlike in body language, but then the AI has had generations—centuries—to observe and imitate. "There is no *me*, esteemed citizen. You are communicating with an intricate set of heuristics, but that is not a self. Function is its own justification and essence. Do you assign personal names to your hippocampus, your pancreas, your lungs? The lack of names doesn't diminish their necessity. And so the subject is Pilot first, as the shipworld is shipworld first before all sentiment."

Suranut can't tell whether the cortex is being sarcastic. "Let me dress."

"Your belongings will be moved to a suite adjacent to Pilot's, where you will stay for the duration of this experiment. Your work will be suspended."

A suite. She glances at her cluttered room: a workspace and a bed. Everything else is folded into the bulkhead, modular and bare and small. "To be a citizen is to work. To be a citizen is to earn the resources to which one is allotted." The most important civil tenets.

"This is work, citizen, of a different nature to your routine assignment but no less crucial."

In the end there is no arguing with the cortex, and when all is said and done its authority is checked only by the shipworld's administrative council.

The fishbowl room is larger this time, more furnished. New additions: a wardrobe, an alcove with a window that looks out onto empty blackness, and a table for two. Last, in a partition of its own, a frame of bars and counterweights that look more like a torture instrument than exercise. Gullaya hangs from it upside down, her legs hooked around the top frame and her body supported by an inclined metal slab.

Centimetre by centimetre she levers herself until she is nearly upright. The muscles of her thighs bunch; those of her abdomen cord, and the cables joining to her the ceiling flex. Sweat alloys her limbs with radiance, jeweling her flanks and throat. "What do you do?" Gullaya asks, words punctuated by quick gasps.

Suranut wrests her gaze away from the undulation of muscle, the perspiration glazing barely-clothed skin, the musk and salt. "I'm a historian. I specialize in certain social movements from late twenty-first to early twenty-second century. Did you know, there was a time when two women or two men couldn't marry each other back in Muangthai? That changed at one point, but even afterward it wasn't so easy for women to be wife and wife, men husband and husband... let alone any other genders. It's so long ago, nearly unbelievable, and it's easy to feel disconnected from all that. To just forget them as an artefact of an ancient, primeval time. But their lives and names deserve memorializing. Their struggles and their deaths. The ones who lived to see their dream, the ones who didn't. The ones who got to finally marry at eighty-five."

The pilot unhooks her legs and climbs down. She is sheathed in a material too supple to be fabric, one that is loosening up into a sleeveless shirt and skirt down to her knees. It leaves her back naked from top to base of spine, room for the cables and the jacks they are plugged into. "The right to die should be an essential, inviolable one, don't you think?"

"I'm sorry?"

"I never meant to return—I was piloting *away* from here, into the sun maybe, but the cortex took over navigations and forced me back here. Every step of the way I fought that; I even crashed, as near to fatally as I could manage, and still they had to revive me. They won't let me die."

The cortex's voice, disembodied: "You represent an unprecedented sum of shipworld resources invested, Pilot. To allow that to go to waste would be wrong. While an individual citizen may terminate themselves they first have to repay their debt to Krungthep. Only then does duty end. Yours is far from finished."

Gullaya laughs, her teeth showing bird-sharp and lustrous as lacquered bone. "You see?"

At closer look Suranut discovers that the pilot is much less senior than she first believed. Twenty-five at most, a long sculpted face with immense eyes that make her look even younger. Phenotype from southern Muangthai base: dark skin, shapely nose. "You're much too young to think like that."

"Wrong. Factor in the travel time and I'm much older than you, Khun Suranut. But even if I weren't, who are you to question my agency? Who's the AI up there?" Gullaya jabs a hand upward. "It even has the *nerve* to tell me to exercise so my muscles don't atrophy. Who the hell does it think it is?"

"The shipworld's custodian, Pilot. Insurance against extinction events."

"Fuck off," Gullaya murmurs, without any real fervour. "You're going to live with me, I hear. Let's show you to your room."

Suranut's quarters are as generous as the pilot's, sized to house an entire family. The walls are warmer than Gullaya's, rose-gold gradients. Half the room gives a view of old Krungthep at night: skyscrapers as far as the eye can see, the Chao Praya ignited by traffic. Bridges over canals and bridges joining buildings. Temples like miniature suns. She imagines going to sleep each night looking at this.

"There were three of us," Gullaya says, abruptly. "Pilot, scout, archivist. Each of us had a different role, but it was mostly about company. There had to be more than one, to keep each other sane. There had to be a third, to counterpoint and hold the balance. The human psyche is a brittle cup, prone to overflowing, to leaking, to breaking."

Suranut is pricked by a sudden understanding: why she is

here. "What happened to them," she says, more statement than question.

The cityscape reflects in Gullaya's pupils, harsh and colourless. "Wouldn't you like to know?"

While Suranut can't leave their joined quarters, she comes to realize that Gullaya has even less freedom than she. The life supports extend more than Suranut would think possible, but they still tether the pilot as though the cortex is weary of what Gullaya might try given half a chance.

Weeks pass. There are days where Gullaya sleeps for eleven hours, waking only to eat. "They don't let me have any alcohol," the pilot would say, bleary, tangled in the sheets. Rolling over and going back to sleep. Suranut is half-minded to simply continue her work; the cortex has authorized her unprecedented access to the shipworld's database, giving her material to mine that she didn't even realize had survived. But Gullaya's disarray offends—Suranut's first sight of the pilot was one of post-human perfection, a creature that expresses what *could* be rather than what is, a tremendous promise. The pilot should at least maintain basic hygiene and so Suranut all but throws Gullaya into the bathroom.

"I'm not letting you out," she says, "until you smell civilized again."

"Who are you, my mother? *I'm* your senior." But Gullaya does emerge clean, smelling of jasmines and mangoes. Those being what they do, indeed, have for lunch: rice from the greenhouse deck drenched in jasmine water, dried fish, pork balls and fried shallots. For dessert, ripe mangoes and sago in coconut milk.

For a change, the pilot finishes most of her portion. "Look at all this waste," she says, even then. "Such extravagance just to feed a couple of nobodies. Adding to the tally of my *debt* to the shipworld, no doubt."

"Not so, Pilot. While you are here, what is spent to maintain you will not add to your total—even if it did, it would be insignificant compared to your existing debt. These niceties are provided for Khun Suranut so she would not give up too quickly and abandon you."

Suranut cleans her bowl down to the last drop of coconut milk, the last speck of sago. "Is there anything we can do but eat and sleep? You can't blame her for being bored out of her wits."

Half a second of quiet, more for effect than function: not as though the AI needs that long to weigh the decision. "A segment of Recreation will be transferred to your deck. Esteemed citizen, you will be entrusted with Pilot's safety and conduct."

To that, Gullaya snorts. "What can she do, anyway? The last ones were all psychiatrists, therapists, and they couldn't wring a thing out of me. What hope does she have?"

"I'm right here," Suranut says mildly. Marvels quietly at this creature who is so human after all—the only person alive who's seen Earth and its impaled heart, Krungthep and its shredded shadows.

The Recreation segment is ready within the next twenty-four hours, the fastest deck rearrangement Suranut has ever seen; normally something like that would require a month's wait, a great deal of bureaucracy, and a *very* good reason. But she supposes she is dealing with the highest bureaucrat of all, the ultimate authority.

When they are admitted, Suranut realizes that this is not the Recreation she knows. The immersion scales larger than life: a primeval forest of high canopies, perfectly green—individual leaves like jade and the sun slanting to filigree the mulch in platinum. Suranut kneels to touch the undergrowth and finds the texture velvet, the smell rich and wholesome. In a corner of her eye she glimpses shadow-striped gold, a flash of yellow eyes and lashing tail.

The only break in the illusion is Gullaya's umbilici, thinner and more transparent but still visible. Even so she belongs:

the planes of her skin in interplay with the shade, sun-gleam collecting at her clavicles and in the dip of her throat. Her talons make a peculiar music against the mulch, the material of the deck module.

"Probably some educational game of the AI's," the pilot mutters as she leads. "An adventure."

Suranut stands this close on the cusp of asking whether Earth looks like this, today. Probably not. Not even close. This is a perfect forest, more romanticized and supreme than any that ever existed. It is ersatz. But—the charred wastelands that pock humanity's cradle, some of those must have healed. In pieces and in stages, step by reluctant step. The most optimistic projection of Krungthep as it is now has always enchanted her: the ruins of skyscrapers draped over with green life, their bases overcome by spores and fungi, pigeons nesting in temple skeletons and the river thick—so thick—with crocodiles.

"There were three of us." Gullaya's voice sends ripples through the sunrays. "We didn't get along, at first. Even the AI in all its wisdom couldn't find three qualified candidates whose personalities complemented each other naturally. I hated the archivist, this mouse of a man, always trying to play mediator between me and the scout. In the end, we managed, and I... what does it matter? Go on, ask the questions, the same ones as the others. You're so desperate to know it must hurt."

"I am." Though Gullaya said *the archivist* and *the scout* with the heat of blood abandoning artery in haemorrhage, she leaves out their names; Suranut does not fail to notice. "But you aren't going to tell."

"I'm not going to give in to, what, reverse psychology." The pilot quickens her stride into a march, then a run.

Suranut doesn't try to catch up. Instead she lets the AI track Gullaya and guide her. She keeps seeing tigers in pieces, between blinks like hallucinogenic splices. "Pilot is unwell, as you may have noticed," the cortex says as she rounds a tree stump. Its radius is longer than her arm.

"Hard not to notice."

"She refuses to be medicated and her auto-diagnostics can recognize hormone stabilizers. Her reactions to being forcibly injected are less than gracious. There was a motion," it goes on, "to domesticate her by drugs and conditioning."

A sick understanding centipedes down the back of her mouth. "You stopped them?" Because had the AI agreed to that decision, Gullaya would not be walking and talking. She would be prone and hardly sentient, dosed into unmoored dreams and vivisected self.

"We have resources to attempt another Earth venture, but it'd be more efficient to have her as a model—a veteran to either accompany or train the second expedition. Pilot has more than one use and ruining her mind for short-term gains would be a waste."

The nausea sharpens, hardening in her throat.

One of the birds has flitted down, red-breasted and red-beaked, to perch on the stump. "The shipworld should have been able to monitor the entire journey, but after they made Earth-fall a series of fatal errors occurred." The AI bird preens, copper wings flaring. "It would be best if you can help Pilot quickly. Human patience has a limit and once that limit is met, no amount of algorithm and cortex logic will gainsay it. The most objective of intelligences, the most exact arithmetic—all are paper walls before the killing flame of human temper."

Suranut comes to a banyan tree. The size of a shipworld, the canopy like a planet's roof. She cranes her neck up and up, toward mirage infinity.

And on a bough the scale of a giant's shoulder, Gullaya stands. At ease, entirely relaxed, hands at her sides. Her mouth is a stitch of smile, her eyes tight shut.

Licking her lips Suranut tries to remember the distance between a deck's ceiling and ground. "Pilot is in no danger," the AI says in her ear. "She's more impact-resistant than most. A few broken bones, depending on the angle of landing, unless she falls headfirst. Still, best avoided."

An assessment with which Suranut can readily agree. The height is enough to give her vertigo, though some of that *has* to be a perspective trick. But more than the height there is the wall of the pilot's bitterness, the briar-paths of her loss. "Gullaya. What did you want to be, growing up?"

The pilot opens her eyes. Their voices carry to one another, as though the AI has arranged the acoustics just so. "Astrophysicist. Only I didn't have the brains for it."

"Me too. Mathematician. Except numbers and I didn't get along too well, calculus tripped me up terribly and then I got far too interested in dead people. At first I specialized in war—the arms races, the negotiations, the catastrophes that led to apocalypse—but that got depressing. I started focusing instead on the people who brought changes. Good changes."

"What for?"

"Possibility." Like the sky, but that is a childish thing and so she does not voice it. "Life in the shipworld is—it's like living in amber. It's stasis. Something has to change or break."

A fractured laugh. "And you want me to be the change, so we don't break?"

"No, I want you to try again. The numbers you couldn't get right the first time, the bits of physics you couldn't wrap your head around. There's no reason any of this has to be final."

"Death is final. Loss is permanent. None of that can be tried again or revised." Gullaya moves. A step forward. A step back. Then she stops. For a long time, she stands that way, every limb and muscle tensed.

Then she leaps—

But she never falls. The umbilici draw taut and Suranut is sure, is certain, they must snap. Instead they hold and Gullaya hangs suspended, a puppet in mid-flight. The pilot starts laughing, long and loud.

After, it is as though a door inside Gullaya has broken down. She insists on showing Suranut where she landed. "If the cortex lets us out of this fucking place," she adds, for they return to the suite to find it crowded with ghosts.

One man, one woman. The man is nondescript, lanky and thin-faced, a mop of unruly hair; the base of his skull is sheathed silver, data storage and direct neural links. The woman is tall and thick-waisted, coiffed and neat. While there's only one of the man, the woman's images are replicated everywhere— seated, standing, hands flung out. Suranut does not need to ask who these two are.

The AI lets them go, opening doors for them, coaxing passages between decks that let them stay out of public sight. Gullaya's life supports follow them, rippling through the ceiling like strange lotuses treading stranger waters.

And then they are at the crash site, as close as Suranut has ever gotten to the shipworld's skin.

Blasted and blackened, scabbed over with globules of machine-blood and sealant. The area is smaller than Suranut expected, epicentre oddly precise as though the AI finessed the trajectory until the moment of impact. The ship itself is gone, its wreck recycled into repair pods or perhaps salvaged for the next effort. Everything has its use, everything must be used until no further function can be wrung out of it.

The filtered pane gives them a view of umbral space, lit by the blue-white fire that the shipworld orbits. The star is visually arresting, but uninhabitable: no planet has ever been found in the shipworld's long journey that suits humanity. Suranut likes to look at this star until the afterimage is burnt into her vision. Half of a binary system, ever-burning, on the cusp of a cannibal event where it and its twin will meld into one.

"By then we'll either be dead or away," Gullaya says, as

though divining Suranut's thought from the smooth glass. "At the very last moment I was still trying to fly *into* that and burn. My ship—the ship that I was—couldn't have survived. Nothing would've been left, not a fleck of ash, a fistful of hair."

"I get the appeal." A finale, total and absolute. Annihilation untainted by memento or regret, undiluted by past or future.

"Do you?" Gullaya runs her knuckles along the pane. "You got the wrong person, you know. She was the one you would have wanted—the scout, I mean. Someone who can usher in change. The fulcrum on which history turns. The catalyst." A deep breath. "Of us three, she should've been the one to survive. I was never the marrying type, but she made *wife and wife* sound wonderful."

Suranut thinks back to the image, projected over and over. Vivacious, even in memory. "I would have liked to meet her, but getting you isn't half bad."

A low short laugh. "I thought I couldn't live without her, but I can, and that's the worst part. This person, this impossible person—a nova-flower, a galaxy in herself—she's gone and I'm still here and I can still breathe. Isn't that terrible? Isn't that a betrayal." She covers her eyes. "Cortex, are you there? Are you listening?"

The answer emanates from the ceiling, a fine haze flowering carmine and lotus-blush. "You are always heard, Pilot."

Gullaya's hand lifts and Suranut takes it, instinctive as she would take a drowning person's. "I did it. I killed them both or might as well have. There was a, a malfunction when they tried to access an archive vault, looking for the last moments in Krungthep—the city—and then they got so sick, their cybernetics were rotting from the inside. It corrupted... Halfway back to the ship, he—the archivist—was already... he didn't make it. Died mad with pain. *She* asked me to end it before she lost her mind like him, she wanted to remember who I was, she wanted me to be the last thing she saw while... while lucid. So I did. A bullet in her head. Just one shot. That close, I couldn't miss."

Silence, then. Suranut's hand is limp on the pilot's. But a part of her is not precisely surprised. The thorns Gullaya wears skin-close, the map of her secrets: it can only take this path, assume this shape.

"Yes, Pilot," is all the AI says in pulses of bleeding light.

"Yes, Pilot? That's it? That's all you have to say?"

Suranut stares at the ceiling, unable to shake the habit of addressing the cortex as though it is overhead, a presiding divinity. "No," she says softly, "it already knew."

"Not the specifics, esteemed citizen. Archivist and Scout wore trackers, which continued to transmit up to a certain point. Pilot's turmoil suggests she feels guilt, either as survivor or—as she perceives it—participant in their deaths. That is obviously not the case. As the shipworld balances the account, Pilot did nothing wrong. But the administrative council would disagree and judge her unstable, fit only for termination."

The pilot opens her mouth. Clenches it shut and through her teeth: "You *knew*—you felt them die—and you didn't do anything."

"The three of you were very far away, Pilot. There was nothing to be done. You were a ship, after a fashion, and you ought to understand. Their loss is felt as a wound in the shipworld's fabric; there is a bereaving, and their names have been memorialized so that subroutines will sing of Archivist and Scout always."

Gullaya looks at Suranut, then at the wall where shipworld presence coagulates in a nest of pearls. "Those therapists and psychiatrists they sent me, Suranut, were all handpicked by the council. But the expedition was picked by the AI. And when I returned without my scout and archivist, they thought the cortex's logic was no longer trustworthy." A smile pricks the corners of Gullaya's mouth. "Guess who picked *you*?"

"Algorithms prevail over human sentiment. Tools must prove constantly useful and fit for purpose." The pearls resolve into spiders, legs rapidly spinning out the cortex's messages in tactile language. The script is Sanskrit rather than Thai. "Choices lay before you, Pilot. Nothing and no one can force you, but you must select. Decision cannot be forever postponed."

The pilot stands. In fluid strides she is next to impact-point and imperfect repair. She pushes. It gives, though not far. "I can penetrate this." She looks down at her hand, fingers clenched as though still caught in that moment. Gripping the gun with which she'd given her lover mercy, the woman who would have been her wife. "And you're letting me."

"Correct, Pilot. In all the decks and corridors, the nerve-ends and nerve-paths of the shipworld, this is the one place where you can choose to exit."

Suranut moves to do—something. Stop Gullaya. But she knows that her strength is no match. "If you step out you're going to kill me too." There is no airlock between the breach and where they stand.

Gullaya looks over her shoulder. Blinks. "Yeah. The AI put you there and gave me the choice. Symbolic, isn't it. What's one more life after I took my scout's." She pushes again, fingers tracing the seam in shipworld skin, that fault-line. "Suranut, what do you want the most in life?"

"I—" She licks her mouth, tasting salt and copper. "The sky. I want to see the sky. Like everyone else really, but it is something *I* want."

When the pilot inhales it is so loud, in the quiet. She turns from the scar in shipworld skin. "Then it'd be terrible to take that away. You want. You should have a chance, like I did."

Pressure leaves Suranut's chest in stages. She pushes herself forward and grips Gullaya's elbow. "Thank you. And let me try again."

"To do what? You did what you're supposed to. You won. The cortex won."

The spiders are weaving fast, a blur. Immaculate Sanskrit

streams from the web, onomatopoeiac.

"No," Suranut says, steering the pilot from the *away* that is irrevocable, "I think you did. Now it's my turn to earn my purpose. Shall we introduce ourselves? You're Gullaya, the pilot. I'm Suranut, the historian who wants to see the sky, and I'm here to help you want to see it again."

Chapter Four

Living in Amber: on history as a weapon

J. Moufawad-Paul

I will try here to make an inventory of what history teaches us.
This will be provisional, modest, but dangerous in that it invites all
manner of criticism. It is based on the presupposition that only the
present gives meaning to the past.
Samir Amin

Perhaps the most widely cited passage by Walter Benjamin is that part in *Theses on the Philosophy of History* where he invokes the Klee painting *Angelus Novus*. In a description that might be more iconic than the painting itself Benjamin writes:

> This is how one pictures the angel of history. His face is turned toward the past. Where we perceive a single chain of events, he sees one single catastrophe which keeps piling wreckage upon wreckage and hurls it in front of his feet. The angel would like to stay, awaken the dead, and make whole what has been smashed. But a storm is blowing from Paradise; it has got caught in his wings with such violence that the angel can no longer close them. This storm irresistibly propels him into the future to which his back is turned, while the pile of debris before him grows skyward. This storm is what we call progress.[1]

The point of this passage was to describe a historical perspective that Benjamin found lacking in the socialist movement of his day. Whereas the Social Democratic Party [SPD] of Germany was demanding that the wretched of the earth look towards an imagined socialist future for its direction, Benjamin felt that this perspective "made the working class forget both its hatred and its spirit of sacrifice, for both are nourished by the image of enslaved ancestors rather than that of liberated grandchildren."[2] That is, in the midst of an emergent fascism the SPD was demanding that its social base look to a future where even fascism could be justified—where the inevitable development of productive forces would transcend the horrors of the present. Thus, "in the name of progress [fascism's] opponents treat it as a historical norm."[3]

Two decades prior to *Theses on the Philosophy of History* the SPD collaborated with fascism by handing Luxemburg and Liebknecht over to the Freikorps for execution after the failed Spartacist Uprising. Benjamin in fact names the Spartacus group as one that acted "in the name of generations of the downtrodden"[4] and thus possessed the historical perspective of the angel of history. Whereas Luxemburg, Liebknecht, and the Spartacus group refused to abandon their focus on the historical immiseration of the exploited and oppressed, the SPD instead turned its face towards progress—on the assumption that a future socialism was secured by an argument of history where fascism was merely a hiccup. Aside from betraying revolutionaries who sought to explode the historical continuum through an awareness of past and present misery, the danger of this utopian future-looking perspective was that, according to Benjamin, it mimicked the very ideology that was propelling fascism on to the historical stage: "[i]t recognizes only the progress in the mastery of nature, not the retrogression of society; it already displays the technocratic features later encountered in Fascism."[5]

For Benjamin, over-valorizing progressive historical transformation could easily degenerate into the triumphalist assertion of a predestined march of progress. The dogmatic belief paradigmatic of the Marxism of the Second International was that socialism was historically inevitable due to the logic of the development of productive forces. That is, once technology progresses to a level that challenges capitalist social relations the latter will be forced to bow off the historical stage because they will not be able to contain the changes that point to a post-capitalist utopia. We find a similar logic, today, with "accelerationism" (i.e. accelerate the contradictions of capitalism through developments of technology so as to end capitalism), but this was the same productive forces analysis that bothered Benjamin in 1940: an endorsement of the march of progress that not only dismissed the fascist version of progress but collaborated with fascism in erasing those who disputed this line of march.

At the same time, however, a perspective of history that encourages a return to the past can be quite fascist. Although fascism is indeed about technocratic progress (i.e. the cliché of "making the trains run on time"), on another register it is about retrogression. That is, while fascism may hope to develop the progress of technology it does so by an appeal to retrograde relations of production: a gesture to and a grounding in a past that never existed; the preservation of historical stasis. Fascist and conservative perspectives on history have always sought to conserve an image of the past that progressives, by definition, struggle against: progress might be privileged on the level of technology but it is definitely not privileged on the level of significant historical change. The average fascist is a culturalist who seeks to preserve past ways of relating and seeing the world in the face of historical dynamism: they demand a return to norms of family, nation, race, and gender in response to a perceived social instability.

In *Class and Nation* Samir Amin demarcates the progressive perspective of history from the reactionary:

History is a weapon in the ideological battle between those who want to change society... and those who want to maintain its basic features. I do not believe the pronouncements of those who claim to be above the fray, because people make history, albeit within objectively determined conditions. In fact, social laws do not operate like natural laws. And I do not believe in a single cosmogony embracing nature and society—even when it goes under the name of the materialist dialectic […] On the contrary, those who want to change society necessarily have ideas of a higher quality than those who wish to keep it from changing. This is because society changes. Those who want to stop its motion must therefore ignore the evidence.[6]

For Amin, whose social-historical context was quite different from Benjamin's, demanding a historical perspective that privileges the past might be a problem. Appeals to an idealized past were used by comprador elements (serving imperialism) to undermine progressive movements in the global peripheries. Such appeals were often contingent upon assumptions that there were natural laws determining a given culture's past and that this idealized past mattered more than the possibility of future transformation. Therefore, according to this culturalist understanding, an idealized past of an oppressed nation mattered more than its future-oriented struggle against colonialism—this backwards-looking perspective would indeed galvanize colonialism!

In this context, according to Amin, transforming history into a weapon is to admit that the struggles of the progressive masses possess a "higher quality" by being future-orientated. It is the capitalist and imperialist who seek to contain change and thus dismiss "the evidence" of the historical march of the oppressed. "To do this," writes Amin, "they encumber thought with so much detail as to justify their refusal to abstract and generalize" and thus seek bastion in a "moral reflection" on the past.[7] In *Eurocentrism* Amin refers to this backwards-looking gesture as a hallmark of the "culturalism" mentioned above, where "[c]ultural specificity… becomes the main driving force of inevitably quite different historical trajectories."[8] The most insidious culturalism, however, is not the kind expressed by oppressed nations and peoples but the hegemonic historical narrative of Eurocentrism that constructs the historical specificity of an imaginary trans-historical Europe, appealing to an idealized past to justify its domination of the present. Subaltern culturalisms are a by-product of this hegemonic culturalism, in fact coded by its overdeterministic logic of "irreducible 'cultural specificities'"––a logic that resists the more universalist, and far more radical, claim that cultures can be open to the future, are transformed through struggle, and that domination can be transcended.[9]

Amin's understanding of historical perspective makes sense in light of recent culturalist appeals to the past and tradition made by contemporary reactionaries. There are the Men's Rights Activists with their appeal to a masculinist utopia that preceded the evils of feminism. There are the neo-fascist organizations, such as PEGIDA, who seek to preserve the "civilization" of a white Europe that they see ruined by progressive waves of immigration. Conservatives possess the name "conservative" because they seek to conserve the perceived values of an imaginary past. Reactionaries are, by definition, reacting to the progress of history by upholding historical stasis.

Moreover, in my previous essay in this book I discussed the ways in which capitalism determines a limit in thought, preventing us from thinking beyond the boundaries of its imaginary. In theorizing itself as "the end of history" capitalism thus conceives all thought that transcends this limit as threatening. Hence Amin is correct in valorizing a historical approach that is future orientated because it is indeed a "weapon" that can be mobilized against the limits imposed by the state of affairs.

So, does the perspective of history described by Amin undermine the backwards-looking perspective demanded by Benjamin? Whereas Benjamin claims that the perspective of an ideal future admits fascism, Amin claims that the perspective of an ideal past is the problem. According to Amin it seems as if the proper historical perspective is to embrace change and transformation rather than seek to preserve the past through the present; ideas of a higher quality are those produced by an attention to social transformation, i.e. the future. Benjamin's angel of history does not appear to face this direction.

On the one hand a utopian perspective of the future ameliorates the event of fascism by dismissing it as an element that is part of a historical chain that leads inexorably towards a communist destiny. On the other hand, a traditionalist perspective of the past justifies reaction and thus courts fascism by a refusal to recognize historical transformation: the reactionary despises change whereas the progressive is open to the future. Perhaps these two perspectives on history—one that seeks recourse in past struggles and one that seeks justification in future transformation—are only moments of dialectical contradiction. Perhaps they point to a higher level of unity.

The struggle for historical meaning

The tension between the perspectives of history discussed in the previous section is beautifully illustrated in Sriduangkaew's *Krungthep is an Onomatopoeia*. To restate the possible contradiction: on the one hand there is the perspective that focuses on past wreckage so as to avoid a concept of progress that justifies oppressive events; on the other hand there is the perspective that demands a revolutionary investment in change against reactionary invectives to preserve the past. But this contradiction is doubled, reflected as a distorted image, in the reactionary concept of history: on the one hand there is the doctrine of a return to "natural" and primordial ways of being (i.e. family values, traditional conceptions of race, "make America great again"); on the other hand there is a doctrine of progress that places the development of technology and unbounded accumulation over human existence (i.e. triumphalist neoliberal discourses of civilizational growth). The two sets of tensions tend to cut into each other and often undermine clarity. How can we know whether an appeal to the past is more reactionary than progressive? Conversely, what ensures that appeals to progressive change do not mimic neoliberal dogma? Such confusion is explored in this story of Sriduangkaew's but not entirely resolved. At best it is troubled but, in this troubling, we are at least exhorted to think our relation to history with the gravity deserves.

In *Krungthep is an Onomatopoeia* the generation ship, or "shipworld", named Krungthep "after the city in which it was built", has been away from Earth for centuries following an unexplained Armageddon. Krungthep is an ark, a massive city-state, containing an entire exiled civilization whose members dream of a planetary sky they have never directly experienced. Generations have passed and the shipworld Krungthep remains in exile, yearning to return to the place where it originated and its inhabitants' ancestors fled.

(A brief aside: I feel it is necessary to make a passing comment about my co-author's choice of centring Krungthep in this story. In the earlier story that began this dialogue Krungthep was the site of a collision between two orders of reality, an "XSF" fictional context where the supposedly fantastic was brought in line with mundane positivism. In *Krungthep is an Onomatopoeia*, however, the city is delinked from its planetary location and transformed into a deterritorialized vagabond civilization yearning for its namesake. The distance between the two Krungtheps is perhaps a distance provoked by my earlier intervention between the cities. Against the worry of the atrophy of thought the same setting is reasserted as a space that might exist beyond the norms imposed by the capitalist imaginary. Anxiety is thus shifted into the realm of historical meaning.)

The visceral opening passages of the narrative concern the search for historical meaning: the return of an expeditionary trio that was sent back to Earth to investigate whether humanity could end its exile. The lone survivor of the expedition is the pilot, reduced to ruin herself, who is excavated from the ship along with her recorded memories. These memories reveal that she executed one of her companions. In order to make sense of the wreckage, the character Suranut is recruited by the shipworld's AI to engage with the revived pilot so as to convince her to reveal the meaning of the sequence of events.

Suranut is a historian who specializes "in certain social movements from late twenty-first to early twenty-second century." She is thus someone whose attention to the past is invested in the concept of social transformation. Despite being invested in the past of a ruined Earth—she is one of those citizens who dreams of its lost sky—this investment is guided by a concern about her present's possible inability to embrace progress. At one point she tells the recovered pilot, Gullaya, that life on the shipworld is "like living in amber. It's stasis. Something has to change or break." Her investigation of the wreckage of the returned expedition, along with her investment in a past she has never known, is thus conjoined with a future-oriented impulse to break from the stasis because her training makes her aware that change is a fundamental fact of existence. Hence her viewpoint demonstrates the unity of the two aforementioned perspectives on history: her understanding of the past, as well as her investigation of the past's wreckage in Gullaya the pilot, intersects with her proclamation that the shipworld civilization must transgress the limits of its present stasis—that progress is necessary.

Gullaya is an avatar of the past. Although she and her dead companions were not literally sent backwards in time they were dispatched to that spatial point where the moment of historical rupture occurred. Earth is the diseased past, the terrain that forced the event of at least one shipworld. To travel back to a destination that determined the current state of affairs is to make contact with the past; Gullaya has become part of the historical wreckage. The dialogue between Suranut and Gullaya thus represents a confluence of the multiple perspectives of history.

First of all, Suranut represents the unity of both historical perspectives: her understanding of the past is such that it is interested in a future moment of transformation. She dreams of the pre-apocalyptic Krungthep and an open sky she has never known so as to guide her belief in the necessity of social change. Her dialogue with Gullaya, the sole survivor of an expedition dispatched to this very past, is driven by this concern. Indeed, at one point Gullaya senses that Suranut seeks to interpret the expedition as a possible momentum for change and asks: "And you want me to be the change, so we don't break?" But Suranut's understanding of a perspective that is both open to the future and driven by the messiness of the past refuses to accede to this simplistic demand: "No, I want you to try again... There's no reason any of this has to be final." Suranut's perspective is both grounded in the past and open to a future of multiple possibilities that must, in order to avoid the easy answers of a univocal doctrine of progress, avoid predictions of finality.

Secondly, the event of Gullaya's return to the shipworld signifies the inverse of the historical perspectives in tension. Those in charge of the exiled situation treat both the expedition and the riddle of its survivor as justification for their future projections: the expedition serves a role in the perpetuation of the shipworld; it becomes clear that the authoritative structure in charge of Krungthep is sceptical of the AI cortex's investigation and thus seeks only to link the event into the doctrine of its projected civilization. Moreover, the expedition's encounter with the actual city of Krungthep upon Armageddon Earth symbolizes the way in which the past is as much a contamination as it is a guide for future action: upon attempting to access the "archive vault" of Earth's Krungthep, the members of the expedition "got so sick, their cybernetics were rotting from the inside." Fixation on the past can indeed become a rot: conservatives, cultural nationalists, and fascists annex and preserve a diseased traditionalism.

But thirdly, the entire narrative represents the ways in which the tension between the two ostensibly radical perspectives on history intersect in the figure of the historian-investigator, are inverted in the problematic represented by the surviving pilot, and are troubled by the social context of the shipworld. So how can we unify the progressive tension? What rearticulation of historical meaning will unify the figures of Suranut and Gullaya? The answer to these questions begins with Fanon.

Through Fanon: the dialectic of past and present

Frantz Fanon was also concerned with the tension between past and future orientated historical perspectives. Although Fanon's engagement with this tension was conditioned by the problematic of colonialism it still provides an insight into the apparent contradiction. In *The Wretched of the Earth* Fanon examines the ways in which the native intellectual understands their cultural history in a context where everything about this history has been declared inferior by the settler. The circuit looping between these two perspectives of history is part of a dialectic that, when understood as a totality, unifies the contradiction.

In a colonial present where the history of the colonized has been dismissed as uncivilized and barbaric, the first radical option of the oppressed intellectual (whether they are an author, artist, philosopher, or historian) is to seek bastion in this inferiorized past. "In order to ensure his salvation and to escape from the supremacy of the white man's culture," Fanon writes, "the native feels the need to turn backward towards his unknown roots and to lose himself at whatever cost in his own barbarous people."[10] The impulse is revolutionary because it is an attempt to carve out a historical space, to locate oneself in a time that the event of colonialism has either ruined or denied.

The future promised by the colonized present, even if it is one that uses the progressive language of a "common humanity", is merely an apology for the colonial present: every act of oppression, every experience of immiseration, can be justified by this bland humanism. For example, a key component of US ideology is the sanctification of genocide and slavery through the event of the Civil War and the Civil Rights movement. The rapist slavers that founded the United States are treated as part of a historical chain that produced the end of slavery and the civil rights of the slaves: the liberation of the latter is discursively positioned as a future logically motivated by the violence of the former; the violence ought to be forgiven and forgotten, the "image of enslaved ancestors" less important than the discourse of liberty and the rights of man established by the Founding Fathers. Thus, even those moments of liberation won by the oppressed are, according to the historical perspective of the oppressors, treated as by-products of colonial civilization. The musical *Hamilton*, popular amongst wealthy US liberals, is the perfect metaphor of this discourse: the white oppressors are played by black actors as if they are part of the same cultural continuum—as if resistance to settler-colonial hegemony is in fact the by-product of imperialist civilization, the only language that can be spoken.

Such a historical perspective is what is resisted by Fanon's intellectual who seeks inoculation from this narrative through an appeal to a past culture which includes a long tradition of resistance. It is an act of remembering through a "tearing away" that is "painful and difficult."[11] My partner, Vicky Moufawad-Paul, in her experimental documentary about her family's ruined village in Palestine, has referred to this perspective as "re-membering the dismembered record."[12] As Fanon writes: "the native is disturbed; he decides to remember what he is."[13]

And yet this perspective is not enough for Fanon; by itself it produces only a limited understanding of the subject's relation to history. For one thing, this perspective is too close to the understanding of history upheld by the most reactionary elements of the colonial edifice. While there are indeed those settler-colonial liberals who attempt to sanitize their past with a "document of civilization which is... at the same time a document of barbarism"[14]—who promote an anti-racist future by appealing to sanitized doctrines of colonial history, who celebrate cultural productions such as *Hamilton*—there are also those atavistic conservatives who uphold the most violent aspects of their culture by appealing to an idealist version of the colonial past. The fascist is as much an identitarian as the resistant culturalist and the struggle between the two is based on a choice between competing and atomic cultures.

The fact that this radical re-membering mimics reactionary appeals to the past is more than formal; it possesses substantial dangers. A past that has been actively suppressed, destroyed, and distorted by the event of colonialism must necessarily meet its limits. Indeed, attempts to re-member an irrevocably dismembered historical sequence can be like the past encountered by the expedition in Sriduangkaew's story: a contamination. Amin's comments about a progressive historical perspective were in fact partially motivated by this worry; he was well aware of the ways in which the comprador elements lurking within a resistance movement could be galvanized and valorized by imperialism so as to sell out the revolution, becoming its managers, through discourses of cultural nationalism.[15] The colonizer will not "blush for shame" because the colonized are "spreading out little-known cultural treasures under its eyes."[16] Imperialism can adjust to cultural celebrations so long as these celebrations do not threaten its dominance; its museums are proof of this fact.

In some ways colonialism *is* a museum, a vast museum that produces settler experts who speak with authority upon the meaning of the cultures they occupy, containing the elements of this culture within discursive boundaries. The colonial bureaucrat is a museum official par excellence: they curate the culture they have appropriated, and distort it through their curation.[17] In this sense, even the past grandeur of a civilization thoroughly distorted by colonialism can be appreciated by colonial experts and, in this appreciation, further distorted. Take, for example, the Mayan Empire that has been a source of excited curiosity for innumerable archaeologists and anthropologists. In *Ottawa and Empire* Tyler A. Shipley discusses a 2012 exhibit in Canada's Royal Ontario Museum "which presented Mayan civilization as ancient and mysterious, a relic of an era of mysticism and superstition so backward and irrational that it may hold the key to primeval secrets about the nature of humanity or the meaning of life, long forgotten by the fast-moving modern society constructed by European civilization."[18] Shipley points out that such a celebration is in fact a Eurocentric mystification that, by celebrating the Mayan civilization as "mysterious" (and obscuring the reality that part of this "mystery" is the result of a destruction wrought "by the catastrophic European conquest"[19]), suffocates the dynamic reality of a people open to the future in the stranglehold of claims about mystery, primordiality, unknowability. Shipley writes:

> In fact, these religious, artistic, and scientific advances were not the product of some vaguely alien mystical force but, rather, of a complex social and political system that was able to sustain a large population and create the conditions under which some people could pursue a variety of activities that were not directly related to survival. The Mayan civilization constructed complicated agricultural systems, which many Eurocentric historians had previously deemed impossible given the supposed backwardness of their society.[20]

When the oppressed seek their liberation in appeals to the past they encounter numerous gatekeepers of the present squatting upon the remains of a history reduced to rubble by the colonizer, the occupier, the dominator, the exploiter.

Hence, Fanon argues that all radical appeals to the past on the part of the oppressed only remain radical if the historical subjectivity gained from this perspective reverses its gaze and focuses instead on a future that, like the imagined sky in Sriduangkaew's story, transgresses the stasis imposed by a present that despises substantial change. In the closing passages of *Wretched* Fanon proclaims that the revolutionary option is to break the colonial impasse and its false division of humanity by founding a new humanity: "we must turn over a new leaf, we must work out new concepts, and try to set afoot a new man."[21] Such a rupture gleaned from a gaze aimed at future transgression is not merely a denial of the past orientated perspective; it is derived from its apparent negation.

According to Fanon, the native intellectual who begins by re-membering the past must necessarily, if they are honestly seeking to pursue a revolutionary historical perspective, realize that this past is compromised. Whereas a comprador consciousness emerges in the intellectual who fails to move beyond culturalism, a revolutionary consciousness is developed amongst those who treat this past as an invitation to a reopened future. "The culture that the intellectual leans towards is often no more than a stock of particularisms. He wishes to attach himself to the people, but instead he only catches hold of their outer garments. And these outer garments are merely the reflection of a hidden life, teeming and perpetually in motion."[22] As Amin pointed out "society changes" and a living culture is not the customs discovered in cultural nationalism but a history open to the future in the process of development.

Thus, according to Fanon, while the grounding in the past is necessary to reacquaint oneself with a historical position outside of the narrative of oppression and its pseudo-progress, this grounding must be part of the re-initiation of a future-aimed historical sequence if it is to escape the tomb of the past. Although the rediscovery of custom and tradition produces the necessary inoculation and grounding to resist various doctrines of oppressive civilization, one cannot remain in a state of quarantine without risking the breach of contamination; combat through new sequences of vaccination is required. Fanon is unequivocal: "The desire to attach oneself to tradition or bring abandoned traditions to life again does not only mean going against the current of history but also opposing one's own people."[23]

For Fanon, the past and future orientated perspectives are unified in the struggle against the present's oppressive state of affairs. As Amin stated in *Class and Nation*, "the present gives meaning to the past."[24] But the present also provides meaning to the future based on how it has translated its past: this is the science of historical materialism.

The weapon of history

Although Fanon's analysis of historical perspective concerns the particularity of colonialism it nevertheless exhibits a universal lesson about the revolutionary understanding of historical time. The past must be treated as a guide to future transformation and, if our perspective is not fixed on the way in which this past has been ruined by predatory historical sequences, then we will lose our perspective. Simultaneously, hope in a future free from oppression that is produced by the understanding that history is by definition transformation—that we are open to the future—must guide our engagement with the past. Retrograde historical narratives are derived by ignoring this relationship: the liberal narrative that justifies all present oppressions under the doctrine of progressive-reformist development; the reactionary narrative that embraces the oppressive stasis of the past.

The problem is thus not found in the antinomy between past and future orientated historical narratives but on another register. A different axis of historical perspective is required, one that registers history as a struggle from those above and those below:

> When seen from below or seen from above, the same reality is often viewed very differently. Two different points of view, which generate two different understandings, and consequently, two different kinds of feelings and reactions, such as hope and fear. [...] The first revolutionary act in class struggle is to recognize, understand and to seize the world from below! We must not fall into the trap that is believing that the bourgeoisie's hallucinations from above are truthful reality.[25]

The past and future orientations are also located in above and below perspectives. The perspective from above represents the preservation of the state of affairs, whether reactionary or liberal, whereas the perspective from below, in both its backwards and forwards gestures, challenges this narrative. Benjamin and Amin's claims about history are unified in the latter.

In a world where the most powerful nations and corporations promote their perspective as synonymous with reality, the retrograde historical narratives—which are narratives from above—demarcate the boundaries of this reality that, as with the shipworld Krungthep, are "like living in amber." We are taught that there is no alternative to the progress of capitalism; even when we place our hope in the acceleration of technology we remain chained to the singular teleology of this static doctrine of progress. Conversely we are told, by the reactionary factions of the ruling classes and nations, that our hope lies in a return to backwards dogmas of tradition—patriarchy, family values, racism, and a manifold of anti-scientific, mystified, and culturalist ideology.

Hence, as the Amin passage cited earlier begins, "History

is a weapon in the ideological battle between those who want to change society and those who want to maintain its basic features." The historical perspective that resists dominant narratives is one that is immediately in conflict with the present state of affairs; the understanding of past and future are unified in combat with an oppressive and exploitative present. What past sequences do we face, what wreckage reminds us of our anger? What future horizon—what alternate historical process—do we realize through combative assemblages of resistance and ruin? In 2017 the Canadian nation celebrated its 150-year anniversary in order to justify its settler-colonial present that will be pushed into the future for as long as Canada exists as Canada: 150 years of occupation, genocide, exploitation, and imperialism. Simultaneously, in the same year, revolutionaries around the world celebrated the 100-year anniversary of the October Revolution: the perspective derived from this historical sequence—including all the failures, all the betrayals, all the sacrifices that still resonate with the wretched of the earth—promotes a different kind of future. And such a perspective, along with many others, is at war with reactionary perspectives for the meaning of the present. Within this war opposing fidelities, subjectivities, and duties are generated.

As Marx once remarked, "dead generations weigh like a nightmare on the brain of the living."[26] This weight is often difficult to bear: we are haunted by innumerable sacrifices; the historical necessity we have inherited is harder to accept than the historical narratives fed to us by the current state of affairs. Thus, it is often much easier to drop out, accept business as usual, and abide by normative doctrines of civilizational progress. We cannot always blame those who abandon hope. Engaging in struggle puts people at risk or, at the very least, exhausts them. Even those who have literally nothing left to lose and are aware of this fact—those who will persist when others are discouraged or bought out—can be pulled into hegemonic historical discourses.

The world capitalist system is adept at socializing everyone into believing there is no alternative. For those who have no hope and nothing to lose, nihilism often becomes normative.

At the conclusion of *Krungthep is an Onomatopoeia* the character Gullaya is nearly broken by the weight of history. Having returned as the wreckage of the past, having been forced to murder the woman she loved who was contaminated by this past, and now being submitted to the surveillance of the static present, nihilism appears to be the only option. But the historian Suranut proves capable in "steering [Gullaya] from the *away* that is irrevocable." Suranut accomplishes this reclamation by injecting solidarity into a relationship that was otherwise alienated by the past's subjection to the static present. "Shall we introduce ourselves?" Suranut asks, "You're Gullaya, the pilot. I'm Suranut, the historian who wants to see the sky, and I'm here to help you want to see it again." In the end the radical historical sequence is possibly reclaimed. Historical hope is rediscovered through solidarity.

Chapter Five

That Rough-Hewn Sun[1]

Benjanun Sriduangkaew

In a time of siege, familiar topography becomes foreign and fluid. It is not a matter of deprivation but a strangeness that's descended like mirage, making a labyrinth of Kemiraj's streets, ribcages of Kemiraj's tapered roofs. The architecture and avenues that Lussadh knows as well as the working of her own muscles, the teeth and wheels of her mind, all have become displaced from memory.

She thinks this as she scales the western wall, up toward the Gate of Glaives. She does not hide her face. Now of all time it is imperative that she is seen, the prince, the king-in-waiting climbing the ramparts. It is symbolic; she performs. There is no grit in the wind to shield her eyes from, that too has changed. The air is damp, vaporous, thawed ice gone to mist.

One last step mounted. She is shaded from the day, which in spite of the siege remains itself, gold-white and lethal. She is also obscured from the sight of marksmen, though conventional combat has ceased months past. For the moment she is not at risk of bullets. Enemy soldiers, parched and sun-blind, retreated ignobly in a disaster of strategy and logistics. Their general is a fool. The desert is its own world, a terrain that has created its own laws. Every last infantry must be armed with comprehension of the human body: the proportion of liquid, when to replenish it, how to tame the demon of thirst. The balance of the flesh is not a lesson foreign invaders can learn overnight, or even over months.

Lussadh puts a spyglass to her eye. Once a situational instrument, subjected to the whims of sandstorms. Now the skyline, viewed from here, is always clear. She peers, expectant, searching. It is not as though her naked eye, however inured to the glare and the terrain, can match the seer-scouts and their paper hawks. But she wishes to see for herself, and they report to the king first, not to the prince.

Empty, as they have said. But toward the vanishing point she sees a trim of white upon the bronze, mantling the shoulders of a dune. This pallid stippling seems closer than it was the day before yesterday, evidence of a gradual advance. A trajectory that gathers speed, little by little, the direction relentless.

The Winter Queen, it is told, does not require food or rest.

Her division of the palace, the wing where corridors bristle like briars, the doors deceptively petal-soft, the walls sibilant with guard snakes. This part used to be different, sombre geometry and dressed panels, but in the last three years the current look suits Lussadh better. It has made her wing difficult to enter, the hallway that separates it from the king's court thick with thorns and bifurcated tongues. The architecture answers to her moods.

One of her tigers is waiting by the inner gate, serene, not especially eager. She strokes its head, its fur passing like silk water under her palm, its ears twitching briefly. This is the entirety of its obeisance, its greeting, and for this she has found tigers much preferable to people.

"My lord." Her aide Ulamat steps from the ophidian shadow, almost as quiet as the tiger. He takes her outer robe from her and bows. "Colonel Zumarr awaits your pleasure."

She sheds her gloves, hands those also to him, and imagines a world in which she may rove about her city without performing the role of her birth. There are lesser cousins of the al-Kattan name, there are those who have abdicated their responsibilities; she is not one of them—ambition and hunger, as the king says, are too addictive a thrill, too delicious a force for those like her and Lussadh. Though the pleasure has grown wan, these past few years. But in a time of siege it is not a choice. Her window of opportunity has passed since. "I'll receive xer in my study."

There is not much to clean off, the weather being what it is, but she changes into something lighter and polished. Whatever the occasion, it is important to appear in total poise. The bloodline of the sun. She wears gold, by tradition, a glimpse of the divine fire at her throat or earlobe. But the rest of her attire is indigo more often than not, save for court functions.

She limns her eyes, a dusting of rose, a line of kohl.

Zumarr stands at attention when she enters, drops to one knee. "Rise," says Lussadh.

"Little has changed, Highness." Xie cuts a narrow figure, profile nearly as trim as a blade turned sideways. Stronger than xie looks, beautiful muscles; Lussadh knows personally. A paper wasp perches on xer wrist, one of xer many familiars. "The queen marches and where she treads, the land alters. She leaves a wake of winter. One would've thought it would evaporate behind her. When we cut her down five days past—a clean shot through the spine, one through the head, another through the heart—she merely got up again, as before."

Three points of severance, simultaneously. It usually kills most things. "I do wonder why it is that we call her by her preferred title." The Winter Queen. An arrogant way to call oneself, but she has given no other. Far and wide, among her subjects or to her enemies, she is addressed only as this. A title, an office, not a name or a person. "Normally you mock your enemies. You give them unflattering nicknames. Yet here we are, being prim and proper about her. How far away is her envoy?"

"They arrive tonight, in I would say six hours. Alone, not any more armed than would be ordinary. On horse."

"On horse," Lussadh repeats. "How have they survived." In the desert the air itself hosts vultures. Carrion beasts in the sky, carrion beasts roaming across the rocks and beneath the sand. When the queen's soldiers did not fall to the heat of the sun, they fell to the lynxes of the winds, the golden chameleons that hunt at daybreak. A thousand dangers for those naive to the terrain.

A pause, abashed. "We think it is some protection bestowed by the queen. No predator approaches the envoy. Nor do they appear to thirst or fatigue." Zumarr does not admit or betray fear. Xie is not a creature given to anxieties. Even so there is a slight faltering. "But such protections are not impossible. A potent alchemist of the spirit can alter skin to endure extreme temperatures, the digestive system to forget hunger."

Lussadh does not ask whether her grandaunt the king has received this same report; it is moot. But Zumarr is one of a handful who do, after all, come to her first. She gazes out the window, at the flat sky. Her room is higher than most, though nowhere can be built very tall. When she goes abroad it is the towers that engage her the most, their marvellous height. Palaces, the scriptoriums of temples. Sites of proximity to the sky and therefore to apotheosis, so much of the world believes that. To fly is to be liberated from the earth, from primate origins. "My thanks. That'll be all. On your way out, can you tell Ulamat to bring me the count of their casualties?"

"Of course." Xie rubs at xer mouth, a nervous tic. "And if I may, my lord, Her Majesty will not want to see you in indigo. It has been—some time."

It has been three years, though xie is much too polite. "I'll take that into account."

Three years since the king had her execute a girl from Shuriam, the land of bone fastnesses and ivory sentinels. Three years since the king had her execute her first lover.

Yet she does not wear indigo to mourn that, or even the annexation of Shuriam. She wears it to mourn her own faith, her own certainty.

But that truth belongs to her alone.

The envoy is called Crow.

As Zumarr promised, they arrive at night. By the Gate of Glaives, under the eyes of seers and snipers, Crow surrenders their weapons. One rifle, a knife, and a sword whose white blade ripples and whispers as it cuts the air. They bow to her with fluid grace, a gesture of foreign courtesy. "I did not think I would be received by the prince herself."

Lussadh appraises the envoy. They are almost as tall as she is, long-waisted and thick-boned. Their jawline is prim, their skin as starkly pale as that of the queen they serve. She searches for any sign of frost, a suggestion of unnatural chill, but Crow seems as much flesh and blood as she. "We wish to accord the Winter Queen's ambassador the highest honour." She grips their sword by the hilt; it enters its scabbard with sweet smoothness, satin-soft. This and their other weapons she straps to her back. "I'll personally take care of these, and will see to it that when they return to you, they will be spotless."

"I would be grateful. The sword is Pious Pledge; it's of sentimental value, and has seen me through many battles. And I'm sure I won't require it in Kemiraj."

They take a circumspect path through the city, down tight alleys where seers' familiars—moths and wasps, dragonflies and detached mandibles—can relay what they see to snipers stationed at high windows. Lussadh watches Crow, their gait, their bearing. Solid, easy. If they are aware or afraid of the snipers they show none of it. But then they would not. Kemiraj has never welcomed an enemy emissary. The empire destroys or takes; it does not negotiate. There are no treaties, have never been. Until now.

On their part Crow is polite, hardly the swagger of a winter agent secure in diplomatic immunity. They take in the lamplit streets, the sloping roofs, the mystic quartz hummingbirds that glint atop lampposts. She would judge that they are surveying with a traveller's eye, connoisseur interest, rather than a scout's.

Confident of their queen's strength, or perhaps sharing her immortality.

At the palace she sees them to their quarters, closer to her wing than the king's. "Her Majesty Ihsayn, Sun-Bearer, will see you before midday." She holds out a heavy, thickset key. "Breakfast will be brought to you in the morning, and lunch after the audience. Which hour would suit you?"

Crow gives her an odd smile. "Truly I did not expect the prince to be so kind." Their hand brushes her lightly as they take the key—she's startled to find their skin is warm rather than ceramic-cool, the way she imagines the queen's would be. "Yours is a country that resembles a beautiful dream; any hour in it would suit. I wish you a restful night, Your Highness."

A disarming person. No doubt this quality serves Crow well in their duties, even if winter bargains from a position of strength. And as Kemiraj never negotiates, neither has winter, until now.

Either way she does not mean to sleep. There is business to take care of before dawn. She dresses; she arms herself. Out into the streets once more, her steps light across the roofs. Zumarr would be watching, but for a time she will have the illusion of privacy. She finds a spot on the mezzanine of a gardener's shed and waits. There is dew in the air, a dampness that might have been welcome once as benison, reprieve from the killing sun.

She keeps her calling-glass close to her ear. Zumarr's voice soon comes through. Her cousin Nuriya has left the palace grounds, intent on taking advantage of the emissary's arrival, the opening it has created.

Like Lussadh, Nuriya knows the city well, intimate with the fall of each shadow, the curve of each intersection. Beyond the walls ey would, too, be closely familiar with the contours of every dune. None of them is raised indolent, and none of them is permitted to do less than excel at whatever they choose to pursue. Arms, strategy, commerce. Even at poetry and song, an al-Kattan must be worthy of their name. Those who do not answer this definition are fostered out to vassal houses. Aristocratic, but shamefully lesser.

There was a time when she might have let this be, allowed Nuriya to forsake dynasty and responsibility.

She shadows Nuriya, moving in parallel. Her cousin nears the Gate of Gloves but does not head straight for it. It will not open this time of the night save by command from the king or Lussadh herself. Nuriya instead turns to a narrow street, from there into the back of a narrower house. To wait out the day, slip out with a scout contingent or a supply train at dawn. In Lussadh's ear, Colonel Zumarr lets her know what is inside the house: not much. A painter and his child. Not rich, not poor, kept in moderate comfort by Nuriya's stipend. A lover, though she hopes the offspring is not Nuriya's. Every bearer of the al-Kattan name watches closely for where they sow, one way or another. The king does not like illegitimate loose ends. The painter keeps to himself, according to Zumarr, and Nuriya has been seeing him for some two years.

She enters from the roof and winds, snakelike, through the window frame. Crouches in a shadow, the way court assassins have trained her, making use of perspective and natural blind spots: where the eye will fall upon first, where the eye will overlook. By function a court assassin should undertake this, but they are bound by word and seal to guard al-Kattan flesh; they may not harm it. It falls to the king and the prince to carry out royal executions. Not that the king would risk herself—she would be accompanied. The blow that severs mortality is the one that counts.

There is furniture in this bedroom, but few belongings. The wardrobe is almost empty. A broken doll on the ground, cracked clay and beaded hair. Pigment jars, their bottoms thick with dregs of primary colours. Empty paint-smudged cups that might have held brushes and pens. Rolls of discarded paper, cross-hatched with charcoal. This is the look of decampment, possessions that matter packed away, perhaps sent ahead in a train and hidden among some trader's cargo. Commerce continues apace, whatever the season. War, peace, stalemate.

Voices through the rough thin wall, from the stairwell. They speak of sedating the child for the journey; she cannot tell from Nuriya's inflection whether it is al-Kattan offspring. There is a split-second decision to make depending on whether it is the painter who enters first, or Nuriya emself.

Nuriya, to her fortune. Easier this way.

The painter would have been oblivious, for the first minute or three. Nuriya is sharper. Ey sweeps the room with eir gaze, visibly relaxes for a moment, before realizing—by sight as much as smell, palace perfumes—that ey is not alone. The immediate alertness, the coiling and readying of locomotion, individual ligaments and muscles tensing. A gun is drawn.

"Nuriya." Lussadh doesn't move from her spot; it doubles as cover. "You know that to depart now, of all times, is unusually treasonous."

"I abjure my name."

"I can grant you a chance."

"How kind of you. No."

The whiplash noise of a gun being cocked. Lussadh and Nuriya used to be close; she knows what round ey prefers, smoke and spitfire. It melts stone.

She also knows, with exactness, how Nuriya fights. They were frequent sparring partners, and Lussadh sometimes let em win. One learns more about people that way, she finds, in their moments of victory.

For good or ill, Lussadh is the one selected, the one made prince. Each day she breathes she must justify her title, or else.

Lussadh does not wait for the first shot to fire; she has the advantage. She throws her knife, hilt first, the blunt weight of it cracking across Nuriya's wrist. Disarm, subdue. She is across the room, bearing down on her cousin. A fist to the gut, hard enough to wind, not so hard it would fracture ribs. "You can still come back."

Nuriya gags on eir saliva. Footfalls from the outside. "Don't come in!" ey gasps out, breathy, but still heard. The footfalls pause. "You don't have to do this. Winter will fell Kemiraj, this is the enemy that'll end us. You can leave, find another life, find even one where you can become a lord in your own right. Unbeholden to any higher authority or destiny. Imagine that, imagine a life other than this. What does the king care for you except as a device to rest her crown upon, someone to take her place when she passes. I remember the girl—"

Lussadh looks down at em; she imagines her expression a canvas as perfect as a dune on a windless day. "I do not remember," she says mildly. "Kemiraj will not fall so easily." She picks up her knife, slices across with precision. No point to prolong the suffering. It is not even anger that animates her, just expediency. The moment has outstayed its welcome; time to hurry it along.

Regardless of the source, blood is a phenomenon. Beast or human, common or royal. The geyser of it, and most of all from the jugular, so much arterial pressure. The painter has not entered: she wonders if he is listening at the door. Through her calling-glass she says to Zumarr, "See to it that the painter receives a widow's recompense." The same as the spouse of any fallen soldier. "And bring me a sack, the absorbent kind."

She unsheathes her sword. Decapitation necessitates more than a knife. There is a saying that no two affections are alike, and that is true, but after killing the first loved one the second is much easier. By her third, Lussadh expects, she will feel nothing at all. She glances up, at the window, to make sure she has total privacy: Nuriya deserves that much. On the pane that she pried open to get in, there is a furring of frost, and for a moment it seems as if it might resolve into something—a silhouette, tall, like the outline of a mannequin. But the ice melts fast, and when she touches the glass again there isn't even a drop. She merely leaves a fingerprint, sticky and red as congealed claret.

King Ihsayn: Sun-Bearer, Ghazal of Conquest, the lord who has added twelve provinces to al-Kattan territory. Even in the privacy of her library, without crown or armour, she is an avatar of might. Broad, though softer than she used to be, imposing despite her lack of height—many tower over her, including Lussadh. Her chair is simple wood and lightly upholstered, but with her in it, by definition it has transmuted into a throne. She sits with a hummingbird in her palm, the crest animal, a bird that can sip from cacti without being pierced by their thorns. "What news, Lussadh?"

"I have brought Nuriya to heel." Lussadh sets the box down. Ulamat has dressed and cleaned the head, lined the casket. Most of the fluids have been drained out, the glistening attachment to spine removed, but best to be safe.

"I grieve eir loss." Said as though the matter was inexorable and immutable, the way dawn and dusk proceed. "Ey had promise and was such a capable commander."

In the dialect of Ihsayn, this means Nuriya was a good spare, had Lussadh met with misfortune or proven unworthy. "Where shall I put eir remains, Majesty?" It is her first execution of another al-Kattan, the one area of protocols she is not familiar with.

Ihsayn returns the bird to its cage, shuts the little door with a gilded tinkle. She retrieves the casket, takes a look, nods. "Have the head frozen for now. You've done perfectly, as always. Among our illustrious family—" Her mouth twitches. "Among that, the multitudes of children my siblings and my nieces have so helpfully produced, you're the gold among the brass."

Lussadh goes to one knee. "That is high praise, Your Majesty."

"Only just praise has meaning. Flattery is chaff." Ihsayn passes a hand over the marble map on her table; ink vectors stir into motion, like unquiet poetry. They usually signify troop positions, enemy resupply sites and lines of transport, the accountancy of battle. At the moment only one vector moves, at the border between the outermost provinces and a garrison town. "Winter doesn't parlay, so it is said. The queen demands surrender, takes the answer—yes, no—and proceeds accordingly. What do you wager goes on in her mind?"

Death by starvation, death by cold. The Winter Queen conquers lands that have never known snow. Lussadh does not expect most can survive the change, the young children, the ailing old. A country yields in life or in death, but it submits all the same to this alien creature's advance. "For someone of her nature the desert proves more of a challenge than most. She isn't much of a tactician." Not that she has to be. "It depends on what she will claim to want from us."

During her reign, the king has had the map altered a dozen times. Ihsayn touches the area around the queen's marker. "Ambition such as hers is reckless; her expansion is hardly tenable. Nations are not founded on simple hunger and bloodthirst. One acquires territory because it holds something one covets. I take it that her emissary is thus far not forthcoming."

"A difficult person to read. The bearing of a soldier, the manners of a courtier. The queen's compatriot, I'd guess."

"And there is an oddity. By all accounts this Crow has never been seen. Not at her side, not anywhere. They weren't present among her infantry or commanders. I watched them rendezvous with the queen; they are who they claim to be. Yet." The king circles her map the way a hunting beast might circle trapped prey. Lussadh understands this: for the moment cartography is adversarial. The next time this map is redrawn it may not be to Ihsayn's favour, Kemiraj's glory. "Her emissary is a secret, I'm certain of it, a tool deployed in exceptional circumstances."

It is conjecture, but Lussadh lacks the information to counter.

She therefore elects to say nothing. It would be chaff, as the king would say.

"Have you thought of defeat?"

Once, three years past. Bedsheets sopping with haemorrhage. There was the option of sand or courtyard, but she wanted that moment to belong to her solely. Between the two of them. How impractical, in hindsight. "No. I've contemplated the conditions that might lead to it, but that is not the same."

"And your courage cannot be faulted." Ihsayn sweeps her hand across lines of demarcation, the reduction of cities and population to paint.

Her grandaunt wishes something of Lussadh, a task, a test. She waits as the moving vectors disperse, the map once more ornamental, seemingly an item that exists in service to the king's ego and nothing more.

Ihsayn is not someone who paces, who fills the silence with nervous motion. Such habit belongs to the lesser, she has said. But she does gaze into the distance now, eyes falling on the shelves where she keeps her favourite books. Not volumes on military history, the rise and fall of dynasties or republics. Her favourites are nature historians, those who study birds, write long treatises on the poesis inherent in the span of coverts and alulas: the beauty of beaks, the monstrous insides of an avian mouth. Lussadh knows because she's checked that shelf. Often she wonders what Ihsayn's childhood and youth were like. Whether the king was much like Lussadh, pitted against other al-Kattan children, vying to be heir. Whether Ihsayn had executed her own share of treacherous lovers. But Ihsayn is at peace, if such deeds are part of her history. The king's portion of the palace is open splendour, tall insulated windows and broad chambers, smooth mosaic floors and soft walls where beautiful aristocrats hunt. A pristine conscience.

"Crow is an opportunity. I want you to do anything necessary to draw them out. The seers have shown me what they look like."

And judging by Ihsayn's absent gaze she is observing Crow in the guest quarters as they speak. "It ought to be no ordeal."

Lussadh glances at the hummingbird in its cage, but not for long. "Your Majesty, I very much doubt a monarch's prized agent can be suborned through means so unsophisticated."

"Do you?" The king smiles. "Desire is a potent currency, as you're well aware. At our roots we are base impulses. There may be an opening to exploit. If not, you'll have tried your best."

As much chastisement—a reminder that Lussadh fell to her own base impulse—and dismissal: *you'll have tried your best.* "I will see what can be done, Majesty."

She calls Ihsayn that, never aunt or grandaunt.

The reception is as folded in ceremony as any other, and like most public ambassadorial affairs, next to nothing of meaning passes. Crow gives obeisance, sharply correct, and does not miss a single title of Ihsayn's. They extend the courtesy to Lussadh. "Prince of al-Kattan, the Dastgah that Strikes, the sword to the crown. To you the Winter Queen sends her greetings."

"Which I accept as host to her envoy." Lussadh occupies her customary place, a seat below the king's. The subsequent one, a chair lesser than hers, is empty. Ihsayn has not had a spouse or favoured concubine for many years. "Kemiraj gives you welcome, and Her Majesty grants you audience." The signal that says Crow may rise.

They do so, small in the deific-scale hall, alone on the mosaic floor and limned in morning sun. For the occasion they have donned an elaborate ensemble: layered silk robes defined by straight lines, secured by a black sash. Their hair is held by a long hairpin from which silver hyacinths depend. Their resemblance to the queen is striking, illuminated. Offspring, nephew, cousins get. That close in kinship. Younger than Lussadh first took them for, not that far from her age. "Winter does not seek conflict with the dynasty of the sun," they say. "The queen wishes for a relation and sees no gain in us bringing each other to ruin, or at least to squander. She regrets the losses on both our parts."

Ihsayn regards the emissary from her elevated vantage, outwardly impassive, disinterested. "What does she propose?"

"An exchange of knowledge. We shall send our finest scholars and inventors to your university, and they will learn from your scientists and alchemists. In such a way we may engage in the most honourable of commerce and come to peace. Winter most wishes to have you as ally."

In other words, spies. No doubt some would be legitimate scholars, but not all. Lussadh glances at her king.

"An ennobling idea that will enrich us both." The king spreads one hand, munificent, as though months ago she was not slaughtering winter soldiers and they weren't doing their level best to terminate the al-Kattan lineage. "I am amenable to this. Indeed the prince shall show you the university herself, and we shall see from there the fine details of our agreement."

Crow bows deeply. "The wisdom of the Sun-Bearer is renowned, as is her magnanimity. I thank you for this chance, Your Majesty."

It seems underwhelming after all the artillery those months past, but then both sides are acting on pretence. Further pleasantries are traded, monarchic praises. Too humble by far, Lussadh thinks, for the agent of winter who may be the queen's relation. Nor has Crow admitted to any title. Hard to read, harder to place in hierarchy. She scrutinizes the robes and attempts to divine their meaning: does the sash indicate rank, does the colour or texture of the silk. But they are foreign, she has never seen their like.

She escorts Crow out of the audience hall, curious to see them move in the heavy attire. They are no less fluid, and they make their wood sandals look elegant. The robes add rather than impede. They are observing her in turn, and she wonders what they make of her, the gun and blade at her hip, the circlet atop her skull. "I wasn't able to have them prepare food you might find familiar, but perhaps you'd be in the mood to try our cuisine."

"I have an adventurous palate." Crow smooths down their wide sleeves. The folds seem voluminous, infinite; anything can be hidden within their shadow. "It may be impolitic to mention this, but I was there to bear witness and I thought you magnificent on the battlefield. Like the red-gold god, who in my homeland governs the science of combat."

"Were you on the field?"

"After a fashion. While I can fight, I was there as a... standard-bearer, if you will, a symbol." Their hairpin tinkles; their head twitches side to side. A fragrance of apple and cinnamon emanates from them, some strange edible perfume. "You fuelled our officers' nightmares. So many sleepless nights given to imagining how you would dismember or torture or behead them. In a way it kept them disciplined."

Despite herself Lussadh almost laughs. Obvious flattery, but Crow is so matter-of-fact about it. She does not press as to what exact capacity they filled in the queen's army. That would be for later.

They have lunch in the river room, the one part of Lussadh's wing that has not been overtaken by thorns and serpents. She has kept it clear. The artificial stream that bisects the room runs and gleams, small fish with scales like precious metals and eyes like rubies, framed by banks sculpted from sandstone. Pots of trimmed hedge and imported anthuriums, in every colour that she can get her hands on. Albumen white, pollen yellow, jade green.

"You must like this flower," Crow says as they sit.

"I'm impressed by their endurance. They aren't a desert plant, but with a little help they've got exceptional longevity. One of my tutors was fond of violets. To please her I tried to grow some. As you might imagine, however much water I squandered, they couldn't be kept alive for long."

"The prince is most practical in what she finds beautiful."

"I am of Kemiraj," Lussadh says. It is an explanation, in its own manner. "What about you?"

"Strength. Not necessarily strength at arms, strength of the body, or even strength of the intellect; I mean strength to resist inertia, to break free from a prescribed path. Strength to carve one's own course, that is what I find the most superb."

Lussadh finds her smile a little tight. Too close to home, too like Nuriya's taunt. Coincidence; naturally Crow would profess to lofty ideals.

Servants bring their meal, covered platters of garlic flatbread, bowls of curry and milk curds, dethorned cacti stuffed with spices and ground lizard meat. Lussadh makes a point of sampling from every dish first, to show her guest that the food is safe to eat, that Kemiraj would not stoop so low as to poison an ambassador. On short notice she can learn much about someone through these simple means—in combat, or at a meal. The manner of eating tells the upbringing or at least the training: whether someone converses over food, how quickly or deliberately they consume, whether they pick at their plate. Crow is, as they promised, adventurous and does not balk at eating cactus. They ask if it was fried in olive oil, how sumptuous. There is efficiency to how they dine and she can believe they have been in the field, in circumstances where meals are rationed and irregular, and must be finished in good time.

"If you will forgive me, Prince Lussadh," Crow says as they spread milk curds on a flatbread, "I expected you would be more extravagant in person. Louder, more raucous. But you're as dignified as any poet."

She refills both their cups. Chilled milk, sweetened with honey. From the rim of her cup she meets Crow's gaze with one eyebrow raised. "Is it so bad a thing, to be quiet?"

"It's a trait that intrigues. But it is not that you're merely quiet. You observe. Ah—may I? I've to redo my hair." Crow cranes their neck sideways, unnecessarily. It draws attention to the line of their throat, to the hollow at the base, those exquisite places that invite the lover's fingers and mouth. They smooth down their hair, repin it. They smile. "I am not used to being the subject of study. Like you I prefer to be on the other end."

"I would have thought someone of your station would be used to attention." Lussadh leans forward a little, allowing that show of interest. Her grandaunt's order or not, she will concede that Ihsayn is correct in that the task would be no ordeal, if she chooses to carry it out. She has overseen torture. This is more pleasant, as far as the arithmetic of it goes.

Crow laughs, a velvet sound. "What is my station? I am my queen's instrument. In her lands many would have my life so they may displace me in her favour. But this is gorgeous food, in even better company. Rank has fallen away; I feel capable of anything."

Over the next weeks Lussadh guides Crow through the city, its shops and gardens, its temples and academies. She does not show them the city garrison or palace defences, and does not mention the seers or the assassins, and Crow does not ask. Zumarr relays that the queen's march has paused, far out at the borders where she has raised a little palace for herself made of her element. Though Crow must be in communication with the Winter Queen, they rarely mention her.

At the temple to the sun, in a prayer room of rutilite tiles and murmuring fountains, Crow asks whether Lussadh believes herself a containment for divinity. "It seems odd to come to a temple when you're the object of veneration."

"We don't literally think we are gods incarnated in mortal coil," Lussadh says. "What we are is a deific contract. We pay tribute to what is above us, and carry out what they require of the earth. This may seem oblique, but it follows a certain logic."

"Ah, a little like priests. Still that makes you worthy of worship." Crow's gaze turns, fractionally, speculative. "There is a magnetism to that which is holy."

"Indeed?"

"Back in my birth country I had this habit. I was a person of faith, I left offerings at every temple, spent a great deal of time praying. I began to notice how self-contained and pure the priestesses and shrine maidens were. That drew me. I suppose I made a game of seducing and tempting them." They say this lightly, leaving it ambiguous, perhaps a joke and perhaps not.

Lussadh fills a cup of water from the fountain, gestures to the prayer basin. "I know little of seduction, but I would be pleased to show you how we pray to the sun. Hold your hands over the basin, like so." The emissary has eidolic wrists. Her body and theirs touch at the hip, the shoulder, forearm to forearm. Lussadh can feel their breath on her cheek. "Summon your closest desires to the forefront of your thoughts." She tilts the cup over their joined hands. "Now you are blessed, and your wishes wheel closer to fulfilment."

They remain in her loose hold, their damp wrist cool next to hers. "And is this all the more potent because a princely demigod consecrated me?"

"As to that I cannot attest." Lussadh sets down the cup. "But I'm curious what methodology is effective on holy women. One day I may find myself in need of such tactics, and as you said, an exchange of knowledge is the noblest of commerce."

Crow's grin is quick, a flash of slightly crooked teeth. "First you approach at a distance, so as not to alarm your quarry." They step away with a rustle of silk and lean against the wall. "You arrange yourself strategically—I would drape myself across a bench or kneel by an altar, if any is available. It's best to look faint and tortured. Perhaps you reach out, breathless, and beg for spiritual salvation." They stretch their hand forward.

Lussadh does not quite take it. She holds her palm to theirs, a millimetre of air between. "And those ordained must give you succour." Their fingers meet, the lightest contact, and part. "Taking you to a secluded, private place fit for cleansing the soul."

"Much like this little chamber. There I'd ask them about yearning, about passion, and guide their attention to—I cannot replicate it here; it requires a certain mode of dress, certain assumptions, to find the revelation of a collarbone risqué." Crow loosens their collars, even so. "Have you ever wanted something desperately only to have it slip out of your grasp, have you ever felt the agony of absence. On I'd continue, quite cornering the poor priestess. At this point I would take my leave, for to go all the way through seems like a terrible sin."

"Considerate," Lussadh says, her mouth twitching, "and cruel."

"I like to think I was helping them preserve their vow of celibacy." They draw themselves up, their posture straight once more, no longer an offering. "Oh. I must ask, as a matter of academic interest, do you keep to such a vow? For you are in your fashion—"

Lussadh looks Crow in the eye, directly. "No, I can't say I have ever considered practising celibacy."

"Ah." Their expression is a between thing, secret, shadowed. "This has been most educational."

They leave the temple, speaking of the inventors and scientists that would arrive from winter. Crow gives a schedule, lays out the logistics, though it is all pretext. But pretexts fill up spaces and populate what would otherwise be blank; they are the ink of governance. The queen is willing to expend the resources necessary to transport a dozen people to Kemiraj who may or may not be scholars. Lussadh bargains it down to half a dozen— easier to monitor, easier to control—citing that it is early days. Crow agrees.

In the evening she summons Zumarr, who notifies her that

the queen has not advanced, and there have been no winter troop movement. Good news, Lussadh supposes, though by now the queen should have withdrawn. Whatever her true intent, with Crow here as her spy her presence at the border serves no purpose other than as a threat. Except Crow has not hinted at anything remotely menacing, has accepted Lussadh's every requirement. There is something winter wants, or Crow wants, that she can't quite yet see.

She keeps an eye on the westering sky. As an adolescent she wanted more than anything to wander beneath it, be a courier who could always be on the move. Transient inside and out, stopping only for rest when absolutely necessary. She'd told the Shuriam girl, who said, *Inside all of us is a second self, one that could have been. We're an envelope for futures. But we all dream of falling, great prince.* Did the girl know, even then, anticipate her conclusion. The way it'd end. Lussadh did not ask before the kill whether there was love, whether she'd ever meant anything she had said. Why bother. A prince cannot be that weak. Lussadh is not that weak. How the Shuriam generals must have laughed, up until the point she put a bullet in them.

She hasn't been to Shuriam for a long time. Little enough remains in it, an array of empty fastnesses. Hardly a country, barely a city.

A knock on her door as she strips down for bed. She wraps herself loosely and when she opens the door she is not entirely surprised to find Crow. They are in a pale, spectral robe weighed down by hyacinths at the hem, at the sleeves. Their feet are bare, white against the black floor, a statue's immaculate feet.

"I'm impressed," Lussadh says, "that you didn't step on a snake or a thorn."

"I have my ways." Their voice is low, a whisper. "May I come in?"

She steps aside. Shuts the door. Crow's robe is thin, nearly translucent. Little is hidden—no place to conceal a weapon, unless it is the secret kind, secreted between gums or on tongue-tip. "Will you want something to drink? I may not—it's not past midnight and still the day of pendulums. The time of the week where one must keep a vigilant mind and avoid all intoxicants." Coitus not being on the list of prohibited acts, which she's always found faintly amusing.

They press their hand against their front, as though to keep their robe tightly shut. "I too wish to be of clear wits. You aren't going to chase me out?"

"You are an honoured guest of the palace. If I can entertain you at so late and dull an hour, I would be glad to."

Crow laughs. "So courteous; so faultless. Someone like you I cannot imagine doing anything imperfectly. Anything." They untie their hair; it falls down, black, like solid ink. "I have a confession. For all my boasts of tempting priestesses, I have never—actually. Not with them, or anyone else."

"Would you rather not, then? We have known each other for less than a month."

They exhale. "I would rather."

Lust, virgin curiosity, something else. They are both in a position of risk, precipitous. Yet here they are. "Then it would be an honour."

Crow moves to undress; she stops them, saying, "Let me learn your attire." Their broad sash comes to knot at the small of their back, and when it has been loosened there is not much that keeps their robe in place. There is no second or third layer, nothing under the white silk and the indigo hyacinths. There is only Crow.

Laid bare they seem to shine under the lamplight. They turn in her arms, pulling the loose wrap from her. They palm Lussadh's chest as if they mean to measure and map it, as if it might at any moment transform into another material—jade, quartz, a vessel of sunrays. "How soft your skin is," Crow murmurs. "No one who thought you a terror on the battlefield would imagine."

Lussadh cups the emissary's jaw. The apple and cinnamon scent, Crow's pulse throbbing in the side of their throat. These signifiers of vitality. "May I?"

Virgin or not Crow is a bold kisser, all teeth, avid and expeditionary. They suck at Lussadh's lower lip—Lussadh thinks of their mouth elsewhere—and when they break the kiss Lussadh's mouth is tender from their attentions, her heartbeat in thunder. Crow is breathing hard, trembling, their eyes bright.

It's been some time since she's taken to bed someone with Crow's anatomy, and there are things she's missed. Like this. "You've got gorgeous breasts." Lussadh bends to them, their soft heft, the tight gathered nerves at their tips.

"A great prince must've seen finer—" Their breath cuts short. Their fingers curl in Lussadh's hair.

Lussadh charts her way down, nibbling, licking. Crow's stomach is a fascinating landscape, a record of their history and what uses they have made of their body. There are scars from combat and training, vivid striae from growing and living. Whatever else, it pleases Lussadh to make these small discoveries when she takes a new lover. The secret curves captivate her the most, the inside of an elbow, the back of a knee, the inner thigh. She attends to that last now, pinching the tender skin between her teeth. Crow's voice climbs.

"Wait." Their hands on her shoulders, staying her. Crow inhales, shuddering. "Inside me."

"My fingers?" Lussadh bites again, lightly, another breath this close.

"*You*. I want to know how it feels. I want to know how a prince feels in me."

Lussadh makes sure, even so. She uses her thumb, her tongue, and finds the envoy as intoxicating as any wine—so much for the prohibition of the pendulum. When they kiss again her chin is drenched and Crow licks it off, this salt-and-tang of their own arousal.

They watch as she oils herself.

Crow's eyes clench shut when Lussadh eases in, and this she has to do little by little. Her own breathing judders at the grip, the pressure, the slick heat. The drum of heartbeats in simpatico. "Hold onto me," she whispers, hoarse.

Lussadh stands with their arms and legs locked around her; the distance between here and the bed is a short one, but her steps are unsteady and weighted. Each movement jolts a cry out of Crow. They fall onto the mattress, and here they are wordless, language discarded. There is only the supreme immediacy of skin and writhing chemistry, the sensation of sinking into one another. Crow's low moans. Her own harsh, high gasps.

Quiet for a time, after that. Noiseless save for their breathing.

"Could we extinguish the lamps?" Crow's voice is glazed, feathery. They lie facing one another, a nest of bunched sheets and sweaty limbs.

She passes her hand down the length of Crow's spine, the wonderful inviting arch of it like good architecture. "A minute ago you didn't seem shy."

"I know no shyness. I desire to see you in the moonlight."

It is an exquisite demand; laughing, Lussadh acquiesces. One by one she snuffs out the lamps by her desk, by the bed. She draws the curtains all the way and stands before the glass, before the vastness of the sky, the shadow-shapes of a city asleep. The moon in full wax, ascendant, its light pouring down like thawed ice. Lussadh holds her arms out, pivots slowly on her feet.

"How is it possible," Crow says softly, lying on their side, "that it is not known across all the realms that the prince of Kemiraj is beautiful beyond compare? What injustice it is that they sing your renown only in combat, in your acumen. But you are beautiful, beautiful. You've branded me from within, you've remade me."

It is only sex, Lussadh could say, you will go on to bed others; it is nothing transcendent. She could say that and tarnish the moment. Instead she says, "When I poured water over your hands in the temple, what did you wish for? Was it perhaps this?"

Crow studies her through half-lidded eyes, and the way they spread across her bed makes her want to grip their hips all over again, begin this frenzy once more. "A little of this. What I wished for the most was courage. When I departed my homeland, it was to leave behind the reign of unjust lords. I desired freedom from the fate they set down for me, which was to be a tool; I desired to reign over my own destiny."

"You still serve your queen."

"In some ways." They smile up at her. "In others, not at all. In those ways I am master of my own wants and goals entirely. Let me taste your lips again, Lussadh. I long to forget everything and remember only you."

Against the windowpane, they merely kiss.

A pattern is easy to fall into.

Lussadh reports to her king. She is thorough each time, conveying all she's learned from Crow, every piece of intelligence. Ihsayn is impatient when Lussadh does not bring anything pertinent, and there is always the threat of the Winter Queen herself looming in the distance. "Winter is turning its gaze to Johramu," Lussadh says one day, aware that nothing Crow has said to her was not meant for Ihsayn to hear. "It seems the queen intends to expand ever faster, and of her existing territories a quarter or so have been consolidated. There is some issue as to selecting her governors, for securing loyalty is not easy even for her, and despite her might she cannot be omnipresent."

Ihsayn has brought in more hummingbirds, half a dozen. All are silent, trained or bred to it, in cages by the window and next to the king's map. To Lussadh it seems a sign of desperation, to have the al-Kattan living crest multiply. It is not strength; it is overcompensation. For the first time she does not think Ihsayn an avatar of power. Instead the king looks harried, diminished. "How does she mean to remedy this?"

"Crow would have been one of her governors, so they say. But of course they are here with us."

Ihsayn looks away from one of the cages and studies her. The pause lengthens, crawls. "You don't seem worried."

"They are easy to handle," she says, more or less true. "Ulterior motives, naturally. I believe that they are hoping to negotiate with their queen. If they can get what she wants from us, they'll have earned the favour to choose a domain to administer."

"They tell you this?"

"I can discern their hints." Lussadh visited the mausoleum the other day, to pay respects to what is left of Nuriya. She liberated, from the casket of personal effects, a gun. Some conquered provinces remember their dead through ash jars; pistols she finds far more practical. "As to what their queen wants, Crow has not yet seen fit to reveal."

"Perhaps she wants merely to stall us. It can be that simple. While she puts her territories in order she can continue this pretence of intellectual exchange, sending us a spy or two, a few meaningless inventors. More comfortable than wasting her soldiers in the dunes."

Lussadh has, for a change, not worn indigo anywhere on her. If the colour on Crow bothers Ihsayn she has not bothered to correct the envoy as to what it signifies in Kemiraj. Instead she has put on princely attire, pomegranate red, chains of gold. It occurs to her that she is not only taller than her grandaunt but stronger, younger. That has always been obvious, but somehow Ihsayn's presence has elided that, obscured it. Ihsayn has ever seemed ageless. Not today. "That must be so. The first of them will arrive next week, and I will ensure Crow doesn't get time alone with them."

Ihsayn's head snaps up, suddenly. Her expression is flat. "Not all winter soldiers were able to evacuate. One of my assassins captured a straggler near the garrison Nuriya used to command. This officer had something of interest to say."

Under duress, Lussadh presumes. "Yes, Majesty."

"I have held this straggler for many days. During that time he has forgotten much. The human mind is a malleable thing, the inner gyroscope of it susceptible to reorientation by force. He did yield this. Crow's likeness to the queen you have no doubt noticed. This officer claims they are not merely kin to the Winter Queen but a container for a piece of her. That Crow functions as an effigy, and holds the queen's mortality. Destroy the emissary and the queen perishes."

She thinks of the white sword, locked away in her chamber. Crow has not even tried to look for it. "My king, that seems phenomenally unlikely. If such a binding exists, she wouldn't send them far from her." *A standard-bearer, if you will, a symbol.* Her pulse steps up.

"It would explain, wouldn't it, why Crow was such a secret. Never before seen at her side. Where else to hide such a crucial piece but in plain sight, in a place where they enjoy total diplomatic immunity. What's more, here they are safe from treachery in winter domain."

In her lands many would have my life. "This is a dangerous line of thinking, Your Majesty. We cannot attempt something halfway. To harm so much as a hair on Crow's head—"

"Tell me," Ihsayn says with a thin smile, "of the wealth of options available to us."

Lussadh falls quiet. There is nothing to propose. It is impossible to suggest the Winter Queen's terms were ever in earnest.

"Your next meal with them." The king herself is never dressed in less than her finest. Of late there is a piece of armour on her, nearly constantly. A breastplate, a gauntlet. A gorget, to protect the throat. "There will be poison *you* can ingest safely and which will leave them delirious for a day or two. We will use an unfamiliar ingredient to the emissary's palate, wind-lynx meat. Anyone would be indisposed having that the first time. The seers will observe the queen and we'll determine our course of action from there."

"And if Crow does not believe it an innocuous case of indigestion?"

The king looks at her. "Then I am sure you'll be able to persuade them otherwise."

Lussadh thinks of what she will wear. She could oversee the preparation of the meal in the kitchen herself, but the king will likely relegate that task to a court assassin. The addition of toxins must be exactly measured and weighed, calculated for the volume of food, the body mass of the diners. When the aim is not to kill but to test a theory, the process must be the most precise of all.

At dinner, Crow remarks how handsome her indigo dress is. "I've never seen you entirely in this colour before. It suits you brilliantly." They reach across and bring her hand to their mouth. "It makes you otherworldly. A vision."

They eat the wind-lynx without objection. After all it is tender, delicious: to mask a poison's bitterness, the meat must be marinated that much longer, the spices must be added with that heavier a hand. Lussadh can taste the toxin if she lets the meat linger in her mouth. She has been tasting it since she was ten, in minute amounts at a time. Building resistance had begun even before she'd been selected heir.

Come evening she is informed that the emissary has fallen ill.

She visits them in their suite, still in that dress they like, plainly attired otherwise: she wears no jewellery. The only metal on her is Nuriya's gun.

They are abed, eyes dilated, chest rising and falling fast. When she touches their hand, she finds their skin hot. Their fingertips feel raw, like little cinders in her palm. For a time they lie there, between conscious and not, twisting beneath the sheets. She calls for a basin of cool water and a washcloth. She wets Crow's brow, their bare shoulders. Even now, she thinks, they are exquisite. Is it true, deep affection to want to sit by the sickbed, and see beauty even in weakness? Or else it is perversion and she has been confounded by her upbringing, and that must apply to the Shuriam girl too. A mind that has not known love can hardly conceive of and practise it.

When Crow wakes, they seize her hand. "I need you to know," they say hoarsely, "that I love you, Lussadh."

"It's the fever talking, emissary."

Their grip tightens. The strength of it startles her. "I'm of clear mind. No matter what, I love you. It is not a thing I planned, yet what can I do?"

Has she heard this before? Did the Shuriam girl say this, or something like this? She can't remember. Recall bends under the weight of duty, the accrued and crushing pressure of symbol. "You should try to rest," Lussadh says. "I'll stay here."

"All night?"

"All night."

They fall into uneasy sleep, eventually.

Toward midnight Zumarr knocks. She steals away, shuts the door behind her, and speaks to xer in the corridor. The queen has been seen, stumbling out of her ice palace, falling to her knees. Not dying, far from that, but vulnerable. Mortal.

King Ihsayn's order comes as night yields. Lussadh paces the suite on bare feet, wondering whether she should pull back the curtains and let in the dawn. No. The sun would be too harsh, and Crow is unwell. Some countries commemorate their dead in jars, in bone keepsakes. Shuriam does the latter, or rather it did, and sometimes she thinks that she should have kept the fragment of a skull or a phalanx. She has never been a stranger to the grip of a gun, yet it feels alien in hand now, eelish or serpentine. Slippery, a thing prone to falling. *We all dream of falling, great prince.*

She draws the gun.

By the bed she kneels and touches Crow's cheek. "Crow. Are you awake?"

They blink up at her slowly. A soft smile. "I dreamed of a future in which I can wake up to your face every morning. Can I have some water?"

"Yes," Lussadh whispers. She fires. There is hardly any sound, so much cushioning. Flesh, sheets, mattress. It all muffles; it all turns a moment that should be unbearably loud into one that is almost silent.

The third time and, as she thought, she feels nothing at all.

The white blade is light, as though it was made from something other than steel. Bird-boned, if such a thing can be said of a weapon. Pious Pledge, Lussadh thought that a peculiar name for a weapon, peculiarly elegant. Not unlike its owner.

The ride to the old crematorium was long, solitary. Still she has made good time. Her beast is not tired, comfortable and loose-muscled in its armour. For the most part she was able to steer clear of predators, though half her carrion traps are gone, the decoys to lure the wind-lynxes and bind the chameleons. Navigating the desert without the protection of a retinue or a train is an exacting science. There are rails in the distance, black lines like a second horizon, but none of the routes come near this place. There are no reasons to. It is a relic, defunct and fading from even the memory of those who once utilized it. There are aspects of a holy place to the crematorium, the finials and naga scales of a temple winding up the spire that vented smoke. The walls stand shredded and perforated; what little remains of the stone is gouged by lynxes. Of the attached monastery there is next to nothing left.

A quiet day, the wind stilled for now. She is safe from the lynxes, which cannot fly or perambulate on their own, dependent on the caprices of weather. Lussadh peers through her telescope in the distance. As the seers have reported, the frost that encroached upon the dunes is gone. The Winter Queen's abode must have melted or shattered. *Now you are ready to be king,* Ihsayn said, *and you'll be remembered as Kemiraj's greatest hero. Historians will never forget you.*

Lussadh pushes her way through a rusted gate. Empty, ruinous. She thought of doing this at the sun temple, but there was no way to safe-keep Pious Pledge there without the clergy informing the king. This crematorium used to be a playground for her and Nuriya. There was appeal to a spot of absolute quiet, away from the monitoring of their retinues and caretakers.

She climbs to the second floor, where monks once presided over funeral rites, and looks for the pot of loam she and Nuriya brought all those years ago. By miracle it remains there, though the violets are gone; they never really sprouted. Ey had laughed at her. She had argued that violets might thrive on history.

The loam has hardened and dried. She places down hyacinths carved from imported wood, birch and cypress, and fresh anthuriums that have bruised from the journey but remain alive enough. Bright, lustrous. Then she takes out Pious Pledge and thrusts it into the soil.

At first it seems her imagination that the air has grown tight and knifed. Then the crack, as of glass under stress. Her skin sears and a roar fills her, as if thunder has infiltrated her veins, her heart gone to lightning.

A hand falls on her arm. She turns.

"I did mean it," Crow says, "when I said I would love you no matter what. Your ruthlessness. Your warmth. Your desire."

The same thin robe they wore on the night they first came to Lussadh's room, the spectral shade of frost on a windowpane, the indigo hyacinths. Except—they are sparer of frame and taller, not so thick-boned, not so... "You are not Crow."

The Winter Queen's head moves, side to side. That familiar gesture. "Even my strength had its limits against this killing climate. To venture as far as your city I required a vessel, and so I made Crow. My effigy, my second self. I never meant to get entangled as I did, but you worked a strange alchemy upon me."

"I didn't—" Lussadh inhales. She is paralyzed. She is— something in her pulls and pulls, she can sense the limit of her tensile strength. The hour between that dawn and now she thought herself transmuted to iron within and without, that she had achieved the final transition from person to function. A thing that performs what is given to it, never faltering. "What do you want?"

"When I left my homeland it was to create my own maps, chart my own trajectory. In our time together..." The queen's voice lowers and then it *is* Crow's. "You may not believe that I offered you my heart, but I did. Now I offer you also the chance. To leave your homeland and make your own purpose. However you decide I will leave to you Kemiraj's fate."

Can it be this easy, Lussadh thinks, can anything? She looks at the flowers and the sword, and feels the heft of Nuriya's pistol. It occurs to her that she has not brought anything on this journey that signifies her connection to the throne.

Now you are ready to be king.

She pulls the white blade out of the hardened loam and offers it, hilt-first, to the Winter Queen. "I suppose," she says, "you will be wanting this back."

Chapter Six

An Envelope of Futures: necessity and freedom

J. Moufawad-Paul

Necessity knows no law besides itself; necessity breaks iron.
Ludwig Feuerbach

There are a number of directions that I could take my final engagement with Sriduangkaew's fiction, openings encouraged by *That Rough-Hewn Sun*: the way in which competing imperialisms carve up geography through war so that "familiar topography becomes foreign and fluid," for example, or the various articulations of gender which demonstrate, as Anne McClintock has argued, how "[a]ll nationalisms are gendered, all are invented and all are dangerous... in the sense that they represent relations to political power and to technologies of violence."[1] In light of the conversation that has developed thus far, however, what struck me most about this story was how it was structured around moments of historical necessity.

Indeed, the historical trajectory of the protagonist Lussadh, prince of the Empire of Kemiraj, is informed by three brutal necessities that are intimately linked to her social position. The first happened before the story begins and concerns the murder of a lover beholden to a polity Kemiraj conquered and annexed: by order of the king, her grandaunt, it was necessary for Lussadh to execute her lover in order to consummate her destiny as imperial prince. The second, which happens in the first quarter of *That Rough-Hewn Sun*, is Lussadh's murder of her cousin for treasonous abdication: her role as prince necessitates this execution, to do otherwise would itself be a betrayal of her social position. The third, which serves as both denouement and a possible opening to transformation, is Lussadh's murder of an envoy—representing the competing hegemony of the terrible Winter Queen—that again is necessitated by her historical duty as representative of an imperial order.

The story's narrative arc is driven by these three necessities, associated with each other through the Kemiraj colour of mourning (indigo), and in a sense the historical momentum of Kemiraj itself echoes the trajectory of necessity that has defined Lussadh's life. Of course each of these three murders were as contingent as they were necessary because Lussadh could have done otherwise: her cousin, Nuriya, who has "forsake[n] dynasty and responsibility", challenges Lussadh to be "unbeholden" to her "destiny". Later the victim of the third murder, the envoy Crow, will echo Nuriya's challenge by telling Lussadh that what they most value in an individual is the determination "to break free from a prescribed path." But necessity is not destiny, though it is often confused as such, and in fact is dialectically united with contingency. Things could always be otherwise, there are always aleatory moments, but if one wants to chart a course from point x to y then certain actions and moments are necessitated. If you do not want to die of thirst then drinking water is necessary; if you want to pursue the interests of your class and national position then various duties are necessitated.

Every historical sequence, both micro- and macro-political, admits that necessity is immanent even if it is neither telos nor destiny. Contingency persists as necessity's dialectical double. Most importantly, though, is the fact that necessity, rather than contingency, admits freedom. Indeed, at the end of *That Rough-Hewn Sun* it is in fact the last act in the brutal chain of necessity that opens the possibility of Lussadh's freedom.

Some preliminary thoughts on necessity
In 1936, the Canadian communist and internationalist Norman

Bethune invented mobile blood transfusion. Working as a field surgeon in the struggle against fascism in the Spanish Civil War, Bethune encountered the necessity for providing blood transfusions to partisans in the midst of combat and thus a method of moving civilian donated blood to the front lines of struggle was born. As the cliché goes, *mater atrium necessitas*— necessity is the mother of invention: despite having become a pithy saying, it remains a simple but good definition of the concept of necessity, where human need intersects with science, history, and freedom.

Although there is a long history of theorizing necessity according to both science and freedom—from Kant to Hegel to Marx and Engels—it has fallen out of fashion, at least in Western academia, in the past several decades. In the analytical tradition the dialectic of freedom and necessity has been replaced by the much more narrow antinomy of free will or determinism. In the continental tradition the rise of post-structuralism/post-modernism resulted in philosophical scorn for the concept of necessity since it appeared to lead to teleological explanations of history: where historical development could be explained according to grand statements of necessity, all of the aleatory moments of contingency were violently deleted according to totalizing historical narratives.

For example, a somewhat apocryphal quote ascribed to Abimael Guzman (or "Chairman Gonzalo") of the Communist Party of Peru speaks of the necessity of "irrigating" the fields with blood in order to bring the revolution into being.[2] Apocryphal or not, regardless of what one thinks of the failed People's War in Peru, there really isn't anything new about revolutionary movements and theorists proclaiming the necessity of violence, tragically or triumphantly, in the pursuit of revolution. (Such pronouncements are no more or less brutal than the necessities pursued by Sriduangkaew's Lussadh.) From the speeches of Mao Zedong and Malcolm X, to the theoretical work of Frantz Fanon, the declaration attributed to Guzman is not as anachronistic as the bourgeois press of the 1990s imagined. Hence the complaints of philosophers such as Michel Foucault: historical necessity is a concept that appears to be less about freedom and more about violent exclusion.

Even though I plan to argue, in this extended reflection, for the importance of the concept of necessity—for the necessity of necessity—and hence side, in a qualified manner, with the statements made by the Guzmans and Maos and Fanons of the world, it is worth recognizing the value of the above criticism. There are indeed ways in which the concept of necessity can become a theoretical discourse tied to a triumphalist teleology. While my caution, here, is not the same as the complaints made by mainstream journalists, bourgeois politicians, and liberal academics (those who ignore everyday violence but are upset by the violent statements of people and movements who have attempted to oppose this everyday violence) it is still one that recognizes the importance of taking contingency into account. A proper understanding of necessity, specifically historical necessity, is one that is irrevocably bound up with its opposite: contingency. As aforementioned, if necessity is not paired with contingency then it will be conflated with the concept of destiny. Rather, necessity must be understood according to historically encountered possibilities that are also contingent.

Take, for example, Walter Benjamin's *Theses on the Philosophy of History* that, as discussed in the fourth chapter, was intended to be a corrective for the SPD's claims about the inevitability of a communist future. By pushing a communist future beyond the event horizon and transforming it into a teleological destiny, and thus ignoring the fascism that was developing in the present, the SPD's future perfect conception of the revolution "made the working class forget both its hatred [of its exploiters] and its spirit of sacrifice."[3] In this sense it was a *false necessity* that ended up suppressing necessity itself: the historically encountered need to, if fascism was to be strangled before it could grow to fruition, break with the state of affairs. We know that such a movement, though necessitated by the time, did not fully emerge when it could have (and *should have* if we recognize, as we must, that the Nazi movement was a monstrosity), for those who rose to accept this moment of necessity (represented by the Spartacist Uprising) were in fact repressed by the SPD and its false necessity, and Rosa Luxemburg and Karl Liebknecht were handed over to the Freikorps. What we find in this historical moment, then, is an understanding of necessity that has nothing to do with teleology and destiny—a moment that collapsed under the weight of historical contingency when history took another and more tragic path—and yet we can still understand, though it was never consummated, that the struggle to overthrow the seeds of fascism in the Germany of 1919 was a necessity.

Hence, when we speak of necessity we are neither speaking of destiny nor denying the aleatory moment. We are also not only speaking of moments that are recognized as necessary for historical development due to hindsight (i.e. the necessity of the agrarian revolution to solve the problems encountered by hunting and gathering), though this might indeed give us some understanding of the concept.

Necessity is immanent, "where every second of time [is] the strait gate through which the [metaphorical] Messiah might enter."[4] If it must be compared to a parent, then it is not only "the parent of invention" encountered in the history of science and struggle, that facticity encountered by militants such as Bethune, but the parent of freedom itself. In *That Rough-Hewn Sun* Lussadh recognizes and undertakes particular actions necessitated by her role as imperial scion, no more or less brutal than the necessary actions of revolutionary movements. The difference, however, is that the latter actions are aimed at opening up another dimension of human freedom rather than preserving what the state of affairs necessitates; Lussadh is acting to preserve her class position, aware of what her social role requires. But it is through such awareness that the possibility of freedom is encountered when, upon reaching the recognized limits of these brutal necessities, a transgressive "strait gate" is revealed.

The speculative concept of necessity

The concept of necessity receives its most notorious and speculative expression in the philosophy of Hegel. Although I believe that Feuerbach was correct in conceiving of Hegel's system as "speculative theology"—just as it is correct to recognize Hegel's role in the preservation of Eurocentrism—it is worth examining this conception of necessity in detail, if only to understand how we must overstep Hegel's idealism and Eurocentrism in order to truly grasp the importance of historical necessity. On the one hand we are presented with an understanding of necessity that is immanent, connected to contingency, and intrinsically linked to freedom. On the other hand, we are also given this concept in a complex ontological system that was in many ways a "colossal miscarriage" because, regardless of its attempt to make necessity-as-freedom an immanent principle, it was ultimately a practice of a totalizing speculative system that did indeed conflate necessity with destiny.

In the *Logic* Hegel claims that necessity emerges from contingency, and that any determination of necessity "consists in its containing its negation, contingency, within itself."[5] That is, those moments that are actualized/recognized as necessity are simultaneously understood according to contingency. Those circumstances that cannot be predicted with certainty lurk at the heart of the possible necessities (what Hegel calls "relative necessity"), just as they remain in retrospect within established necessities (what Hegel calls "absolute necessity"). For example, returning to the example of the Spartacist Uprising, we can say that the possible/relative necessity of succeeding in this insurrection was overwhelmed by circumstances that prevented the possibility of the necessity of ending fascism from taking shape. Similarly we can say that the defeat of fascism was an absolute necessity because it was actualized, accomplished and determined within a historical moment, but even still we recognize the possibility of this non-accomplishment which still signifies the importance of the necessity (i.e. alternate historical fictions about a different historical path where the Axis was victorious, such as Philip K. Dick's *Man in the High Castle*, serve to demonstrate the importance of the established necessity).

But enough of Hegel's *Logic*. Since I'm a historical materialist, I'm not inclined to disappear down the rabbit hole of ontological speculation. Instead, I'm more interested in those moments in Hegel where the concept of necessity, though still steeped in the speculative categories of the *Logic*, move closer to non-mystified articulation. The *Philosophy of Right* is where Hegel lays out a doctrine of freedom-as-necessity which simultaneously contains an understanding of freedom-as-contingency: the former is a positive freedom, a freedom *to*; the latter is a negative freedom, a freedom *from*. Here necessity is also understood as essential to science—since the content of science has to do with "the *necessity of the thing*"—though when Hegel writes "science" he means his *Logic*.[6] Even still, if we are to step outside of his speculative system, a mystified and totalizing metaphysics misconceived as the ultimate science, there may be something about necessity that we can ascribe to a materialist and modern definition of science—but I will discuss this later. For the moment, I'm simply interested in how he connects necessity to freedom.

Since necessity is understood according to its inverse, contingency, Hegel's first articulation of freedom is one that exists in the continuum of the finite and bad infinite: the negative freedom of "arbitrariness" where "the content is not determined as mine by the nature of my will, but by *contingency*."[7] While this is some sort of freedom, it remains a pseudo-freedom: it is the freedom of the child who arbitrarily rejects all boundaries. It is not about willing what is rational but instead a focus on one's own particularity, to do whatever one might wish without thought to anyone else or rationality. The "free" act of a child devouring buckets full of Halloween candy just because they can—Hegel refers to this as a "perverse" freedom.[8] Here, one is not properly free because one is ultimately at the mercy of one's drives, failing to apprehend the contingent nature of these drives.

Following the *Logic*, Hegel's understanding of necessity in the *Philosophy of Right*, while "totalizing" (for it is indeed part of a total speculative system), is not entirely teleological: it is not that pseudo-necessity where what is *necessary* is that which is *predestined*, i.e. necessity is not that which will necessarily come about because of a mystic argument of history. For Hegel, "the only thing that is necessary is to live *now*; the future is not absolute, and it remains exposed to contingency."[9] Since the future can take multiple paths we can only speak of what is necessary to try and secure one particular path in the present as a possible (formal) necessity, and that which did secure a particular path in retrospect as an actual (real) necessity. This immanence of necessity contains some interesting corollaries, especially if necessity is intrinsic to a proper understanding of freedom. In the realm of practical action in which freedom operates, then, it is indeed quite possible that the necessity glimpsed in "the immediate present can justify a wrong action."[10] I recognize, for example, the need to eat in order to survive but, lacking the means, I commit the "wrong" (meaning, according to Hegel's category of abstract right, simply a violation of the pre-moral and pre-ethical right of property) of stealing food. Despite violating the right of property and acting "wrongly" I have still, according to Hegel, acted in line with the law of necessity and exercised my freedom. Indeed, refusing to recognize the moral necessity of acting according to such a visceral necessity would, for Hegel, be an "omission" that "would in turn involve committing a wrong... namely the total negation of the existence of freedom."[11] In this sense, necessity reveals the contingency of simplistic laws banning theft, which may in fact—without a broader understanding of what freedom means—function to inhibit freedom. Only by grasping necessity can we understand freedom in a fuller sense.

Here we can realize how a conception of freedom based on contingency can cannibalize the idea of freedom itself: when it annihilates necessity. In one sense I am free to reject any law of necessity but to do so would in fact turn against my freedom. For example, it is necessary for me to drink water in order to live, and yet it is quite possible for me to embrace an irrational freedom that denies myself water. Am I freer for doing so? In one sense this is an act of free will, since I am making the conscious choice of denial simply because I can; in another sense, though, this is a massive denial of freedom since I am ultimately choosing to prevent myself from being free in the future—by destroying the organic basis upon which I can be a free agent. In a less visceral sense, similar rejections of freedom are made in the terrain of the sciences: on the one hand I am free to reject modern biology in favour of phrenology, but such a choice does not imply a larger sense of freedom—that is, a freedom that is open to the future— for either myself or humanity as a whole when it locks me into the confines of racist physiognomy.

Since Hegel's conception of necessity in his examination of *right* is intrinsically bound to freedom, we should be able to understand, beyond Hegel, his conception of contingency-necessity in the *Logic*. The possible or relative necessities are thus understood as *necessity* because they are glimpsed in accordance with freedom... and, in this sense, absolute necessity can mean only one thing: the establishment of freedom. While Hegel himself was singularly unable to declare the meaning of this freedom beyond his doctrine of right, based on an idealist conception of his own time and place, there is something that slips beyond the boundaries of his system, a conception of freedom in relation to a larger and more materialist understanding of reality, that speaks to a richer understanding of necessity.

For example, we understand the possible necessity of the Spartacist Revolt, and celebrate the absolute necessity of the defeat of fascism, because we know that fascism is a moment of unfreedom. Hegel can tell us nothing convincing about why we would think this way, let alone why it is a necessity, because this requires a more materialist understanding of necessity. It is interesting to note that Hegel made the same charge of Kant, arguing that there was something missing in his philosophy of morality: duty was claimed as the basis of moral action but what, Hegel wondered, was the basis of duty? Without an ethical ground, he concluded, Kant's moral philosophy was an *"empty formalism... an empty rhetoric of duty for duty's sake."*[12] Indeed, the necessities undertaken by Lussadh in *That Rough-Hewn Sun* while not "duty for duty's sake" are duty for the sake of her empire—but why should she care about the duties necessitated by this empire beyond an appeal to the empire itself and her role therein? Only because necessity is mystified, conceived as destiny. Despite the fact that Hegel dialectically pairs necessity with contingency there is still something of the predestined and teleological in his philosophy: Lussadh is a Hegelian agent until her last encounter with necessity.

Hegel's understanding of necessity is thus bound up in a doctrine that, as aforementioned, Marx and Engels characterized as a "colossal miscarriage". His claims about the property basis of abstract right are far from convincing: only ideologues of imperial capitalism imagine that "the absolute *right of appropriation* which human beings have over things"[13] is intrinsic to freedom. Marx and Engels would soon critique the right of appropriation's inherent relation to the capitalist order where exploitation through waged labour, a visceral manifestation of unfreedom, was not at all a violation of contract.

In the *Philosophy of Right* Hegel is consistently stymied by the problem of value, by an inability to grasp the movement of society and history outside of his categories of the Absolute and Spirit. The doctrine of necessity is hence the science of the spirit grasped in its total movement of working itself out according to the Absolute. The multiple determinations of necessity, if comprehended in accordance with objective existence, permit universal Idealizations that speak to this Absolute: this is an idealist definition of necessity, a speculative scaffolding of political right, that despite its resistance to teleology still runs close to the problem of predestination—where the ethical life, enshrined in the state, becomes a historical destiny for those societies that wish to be truly free. If we were to talk about materialist determinations of necessity, of the way in which the concept of necessity appears in a real and profane history that rejects all attempts at mystification, we require a different theoretical terrain. Indeed, such a terrain is necessitated by a materialist worldview: class struggle.

For Hegel, and in a notorious passage of the *Philosophy of Right*, "[t]he state consists of the march of God in the world,"[14] the space of ultimate necessity where freedom is actualized. That is, the state is necessitated by the idea of freedom, the culmination of the free will promised in abstract right and morality. But if the state, as the Marxist tradition would proclaim most coherently with Lenin, is in fact a machine of class domination then necessity in this particular sense loses its claim to a totality beyond classes: a given state is defined by the domination of a specific social class. In this sense it might be a necessity for the class in power to retain its autonomy, but it should be recognized as contingent for those who are dominated by this class. In fact, it is a necessity that the dominated recognize the contingency of their domination! But in order to get to this understanding of necessity, where the mystical shell is stripped from the rational kernel, we must wrench this talk of necessity away from Hegel's speculative theology.

Demystified necessity

If we strip the concept of necessity from Hegel's mystified categories—while retaining what Marx called "the rational kernel"—it is possible to understand its significance according to an entirely profane content. It is not as if such a reading is completely in contradiction with what Hegel established, but it does encourage us to step outside of his system. That is, if we transform necessity into a conceptual category that finds its content in historically encountered need, we begin to approach a far more material understanding of the concept.

Take, for example, this very simple (and yet simultaneously visceral) conditional that was noted in the previous sections: if I do not drink water then I cannot live. Such a conditional forms part of the material ground of necessity; it does not require Hegel's logical categories in order to be understood. That is, you do not have to read either the *Logic* or *Philosophy of Right* to recognize that there are bare necessities upon which life is contingent, and that these necessities are not a matter of philosophical speculation but contain materialist stakes. Before we even begin speaking of the ways in which these unconditioned necessities are mediated by the larger realm of necessity (class struggle as the motor of history) it should be quite simple to grasp why freedom is bound up with necessity when the latter is understood in its crudest materialist sense.

To persist as a living being I require a variety of things that necessitate this existence: water, food, shelter—the material ground of organic life. What necessitates the human being, and thus human freedom? At the very least this profane material foundation of organic need; at the most, if we want to go down the path of locating something unique to the human species (which may be a philosophical labyrinth due to the debates over the meaning of the subject that still hamper philosophy), we might be able to conceptualize more core needs that contribute to the conceptualization of necessity as material existence—but I'm not interested, here, in entering into that argument. Rather, my point is that the immanence of necessity should be recognized as something that is wholly material: if we decide that living is necessary, then there are very clear and material things that are required for life to be life. Existence without food and water is not a bare contingency (anyone who chooses such a life will eventually cease to exist) but is rather contingent upon the necessity of consuming food and water.

In order to live I must at least necessarily perform very particular actions. But how, then, is freedom implicated by this non-speculative understanding of necessity? On the level of individual needs satisfaction, the answer is actually quite simple: any limits that prevent the fulfilment of these needs is oppressive and freedom is indeed realized in acting on the necessity to transgress these limits. For instance, in the most extreme example of slavery (which is, by definition, the antithesis of freedom) the individual slave's needs are circumscribed by the slaver—for the latter controls the entire existence, and holds the right of even life, over the former—and so freedom for the slave is the necessity of overthrowing slavery. In less extreme examples, then, we should be able to recognize the same pattern: if something limits someone's ability to flourish as a someone, to live a life where the very needs of living are not relations of domination and exploitation, then it becomes a necessity to transgress these limits if freedom is to be actualized. If someone or some structure is preventing my access to food, water, or shelter, then my freedom can only exist in securing this access. In this sense, being forced to pay for what is necessary for the bare subsistence of my species' life—the fact that my existence is contingent upon commodity relations—ought to be understood as oppressive; the overcoming of this facticity is necessary in order to pursue freedom. Hence, understanding necessity is the basis of freedom.

Things become more complex, however, when we try to understand the relationship of necessity and freedom in a larger, historical sense: that is, when we are dealing with social classes and political movements. Class positions impose their own necessities outside of bare human life and such necessities are part of the march of history—keeping in mind, of course, the qualifications made about this "march of history" in the fourth chapter. In this social sense freedom is discovered through understanding the limits imposed by historically mediated necessity and the transgression these limits.

Let us return, briefly, to Sriduangkaew's *That Rough-Hewn Sun*. The necessities encountered by Lussadh are not the necessities of eating and drinking (though she would encounter those) but the determinations of her social class: if she is to persist as a prince within her empire then she must perform certain acts, some of which are quite brutal, to ensure her position as a princely subject. In one sense if she is to have a free life *as* a prince she has to pursue her duty according to the necessities inherent in this social role, the most brutal of which are the execution of enemies and traitors regardless of her personal feelings. And yet, at the same time, she encounters the necessity, outside of her class position, of being a free subject: the rejection of princely destiny, the possible supersession of the very particular necessity of her class that might in fact represent a deeper human necessity. It is Lussadh's last consummation of her class necessity that opens the possibility of freedom.

The kingdom of necessity

The fact that necessity is historically/socially mediated indicates a deeper sense of the concept of necessity: limits imposed by moments of necessity can *necessarily be overcome* and, in this since, barriers presented by necessity themselves necessitate transgression. In *Anti-Duhring* Engels defines freedom as, "the control over ourselves and over external nature, a control founded on knowledge of natural necessity; it is therefore necessarily a product of historical development."[15] For Engels (and Marx), necessity is meant to indicate human need on a scale that is larger than the individual level. If we want to prevent the environmental devastation of this world, for example, then we as humans need to do something about the pollution we generate. We understand the necessity to do something about pollution (and have the freedom not to do anything about it), and we should also understand that we will be freer by engaging with this problem. An environmentally devastated world, one can argue, results in a state of less freedom: if the entire world were to revert into another ice age, which is now becoming more and more possible, people would be living with less autonomy—we would not have the same freedom to enjoy existence. By the same logic, those who live in areas of the world where bare necessity forces them to work for longer hours at higher rates of exploitation are less free than those of us who live privileged lives in the centre of capitalism. Due to this understanding of necessity Engels claims "if the whole of modern society is not to perish, a revolution in the mode of production and distribution must take place, a revolution which will put an end to all class distinctions."[16] Since these class distinctions limit human freedom, if we want to be free then we need to abolish such distinctions altogether.

The deprivation of food, or even the deprivation of freedom of mobility (whether this mobility is realized in a car or a train), is indeed a situation where freedom is recognized in the necessity to overcome this deprivation. On the historical stage, then, any society that places such limits is a society that hampers freedom. A society (*our* society) that sequesters our freedom in the arbitrary world of market choices, imposing alienating necessities, is simultaneously a society that, by forcing us to pay for needs satisfaction, must necessarily be transgressed in order for freedom to be realized.

In a much larger sense, though, our understanding of freedom develops historically due to our engagement with necessity. Take, for example, the Saint-Domingue Slave Revolution led by Toussaint L'Ouverture at the end of the eighteenth century: an understanding of the need for liberty and equality, expropriated from the French Revolution of the motherland that was simultaneously the prime colonizing force in Haiti, was bound up with the necessity for revolution. If this revolution was not pursued, then the values of liberty and equality proclaimed by the French Revolution would not be experienced by the enslaved population of Haiti. So here we have a chain of historical necessity: in one moment the French masses encounter the limits of their society and proclaim the necessity of their freedom in the slogan of liberty, equality, fraternity; in the following moment, the masses oppressed by a French colony take up the same slogan to necessitate anti-colonial freedom. The pursuit of freedom is indeed, to use Engels' terminology, "necessarily a product of historical development." This is not to say that the Saint-Domingue Revolution was simply contingent upon the French Revolution (we can imagine an alternate history where it erupted before the French masses were mobilized by the Jacobins) but only that, in retrospect, it did accord to established necessity.

What is most important, here, is the way in which historical struggles against oppression have conceived of themselves as moments where the problematic of necessity is, in some ways, viscerally grasped. Mao expands on the connection between freedom and necessity when he writes that freedom is much more than simply "the understanding of necessity." Rather, human freedom should be conceived as "the understanding of necessity *and* the transformation of necessity... When you discover a law, you must be able to apply it, you must create the world anew... It won't do just to understand necessity, we must also transform things."[17] Understanding that one is enslaved, and then publishing political tracts lamenting this enslavement rather than attempting to transform the situation of enslavement, is not complete freedom. Better yet, as the revolution in the colonies of Saint-Domingue would illustrate: take the axiom of the French Revolution, apply it to the context of oppression in Haiti, and create that world anew. On the historical stage every pursuit of necessity is a grand gesture towards freedom. Or, as Engels puts it elsewhere, an "ascent... from the kingdom of necessity to the kingdom of freedom."[18]

The necessitated subject

Reflection upon necessity is what leads the character of Lussadh towards a transgression of the "kingdom of necessity" that has been imposed by the social relations within which she operates. In her encounter with the third moment of necessity, in the sequence leading up to her poisoning of the envoy Crow who has also become her lover, she is already making gestures towards this transgression. She begins to see her grandaunt, the king, as "harried" and "diminished", no longer "an avatar of power." Even still she follows the necessity of princely duty and murders Crow.

The final murder reveals, however, that Crow was merely an "effigy", a "second self", of the Winter Queen. When the Winter Queen herself manifests Lussadh's world is cracked open, the necessities imposed by her social order breached, and the possibility of breaking with destiny is presented. Earlier, Lussadh remembered that the lover she murdered before *That Rough-Hewn Sun* began told her that "[i]nside all of us is a second self, one that could have been. We're an envelope for futures." The murder of the Winter Queen's "second self" unlocks the possibility of Lussadh's "second self", a historical trajectory and a new chain of necessities that *can* be. Necessity is an invitation for reinvention.

Of course, such a historical trajectory and Lussadh's possibility of freedom are mediated by the fact that they are unlocked only in another imperial order. The Winter Queen is a literalization of Hegel's "march of God in the world" and thus is not a space where domination is revealed as contingent, a state of affairs that itself necessitates transgression. We are merely presented with the necessities encountered by ruling class subjects; the masses that live and toil under both regimes largely remain voiceless. (What of the painter and child supported by Nuriya, the cousin murdered by Lussadh? They remain pushed to the margins of the imperial order; the child is literally rendered voiceless through sedation—*and this is the point.*) Since *That Rough-Hewn Sun* is a prequel story to Sriduangkaew's novel *Winterglass* even Lussadh's transgression of her kingdom of necessity will be bittersweet.

Narrative concerns aside, the three moments of necessity that form the structure of this story are significant in that they demonstrate the ways in which the encounter of necessity determine historical trajectory: doubled with the contingency of "second selves", pointing towards freedom, establishing at every moment a subject who can only be a subject through its recognition of necessity. To imagine history shorn from necessity is to imagine mindless chaos where freedom is impossible: to be subordinated to pure contingency is to live within a lottery, where one can never know or understand what actions will result in a desired outcome. Rather, historical necessity represents "an envelope for futures." In this sense, if we are ever to break free from the limits imposed by the capitalist imaginary, then we must follow a path akin to the one charted by Lussadh: through an understanding of the necessities imposed by our historical conjuncture we must struggle to render every moment the "strait gate" through which another reality will emerge.

Afterword – Authorial Intentionality

Benjanun Sriduangkaew

There is no such thing as apolitical art; nothing is made in a vacuum. This is something I believe in very strongly, and my collaboration in the book you're reading has sprung out of this belief. As a writer of fiction it's exceptionally rare to participate in responses to your work, least of all in responses this thoughtful and incandescent: I have called Moufawad-Paul's *Austerity Apparatus* as precise as a bullet, and reading his considered essays that combine his area of specialty and my fiction has been an experience in epiphanies.

I want to talk about intentionality a little.

The stories included in this book are of some range. One is fabulist, the next speculative toward a distant and devastated future, and the last a fable of power and governance done in the mode of Asian epics. Each has been written intentionally: this might seem a tautology—of course fiction is written intentionally rather than manifesting out of the ether unattached to any idea or person. What I mean rather is that some writers ascribe more staunchly to the idea of apolitical art than others. They set out to tell a story as both the means and end, a school of thought that operates from the assumption that it is possible for art to be anything but a product of its creator and its context. What is inevitable is that something of the writer's ideology comes through, whether it is one's worldview on authority or capitalism, or which group of people is more human than others. Who you are and what you think saturate what you make. Nobody can escape this, and what is thought of as apolitical merely means it is part of the unmarked default (while the subaltern is the one marked as political, message fiction, "has an agenda"). And there's something to be said for art that is made with a political or ideological intent from the ground up, and it can be so without crossing the line into polemic or propaganda. Intentionality is a measure of conviction. (Whether one needs to declare one's intent behind each work of fiction is a different point—I prefer not to—but that's its own tangent.)

Writers are frequently flawed; many of us simultaneously believe in the power of stories but also wish to peddle the concept that stories can just be stories—this is an adventure novel, this is a fantasy about wizards and dragons, here is a love story between a love-struck intern and the billionaire who finds her irresistible. There is an odd disregard to what your story might say about you or what you think: that it doesn't mean anything when your doorstop epic uncritically touts the authority of absolute monarchs, or when every woman in the story is sexually brutalized, or when all the murderous monsters happen to be black while the wily counsellors all happen to have "slanted eyes". Citing Chimamanda Ngozi Adichie's TED talk, "The Danger of a Single Story", may be overdone, but while the lesson it delivers is frequently quoted few writers take anything away from it (that stories do have power, yes, but not just because they teach children to love reading—stories can nudge beliefs, affirm existing ones, can shape an entire continent like Africa in the eye of a reader who has never visited it). When you believe stories can just be stories, that there's nothing revealing or politically fraught about creating narrative spaces where the only victors belong to an empowered hegemony, you inevitably reiterate the dominant discourse. In other words, writers who don't think of intentionality will almost always uphold the status quo.

What I find unique and critically necessary about Moufawad-Paul's engagement with my work is that it reveals aspects of my work that are surprising even to me; they are not counter-readings or conventional literary criticism, but they peer well beneath the surface that I present, and incorporate my fiction into a framework of radical philosophy. It engages with that intentionality: the first story *We Are All Wasteland On the Inside* becomes a framework for limits on the imagination and ideological movements, *Krungthep is an Onomatopoeia* serves as an analogy on the weaponization of the past (and incorporates one of my favourite post-colonialist theorists, Frantz Fanon), while *That Rough-Hewn Sun* provides material for a discussion of liberation and social order. It's very different from what I'm used to as a writer—which is a model of a finished product being analysed and reviewed—and is instead a collaboration; one story results from the earlier engagement, and the parts that form this text as a whole inform each other intricately.

It's a startling, exciting experience to have as a writer, and it's something I feel deeply about. I don't declare my authorial intention, but what I would like is that the dialogue between my fiction and his exploration will exert the same force on the reader that it did on me.

Endnotes

Foreword

1. Meillassoux, 6.
2. See *The Number and the Siren*.
3. Cited in Morera, 71.
4. In fact I use this story as an analogical device in another project, *The Denouement Machine*. It was in fact my use of *Comet's Call* while drafting that manuscript that prompted me to pursue this project with Sriduangkaew.
5. The Zone was the name for the strange region that resulted from alien intervention in the Strugatsky Brothers' *Roadside Picnic* (adapted by Tarkovsky as *Stalker*) and has spawned a small subgenre within SFF that includes M. John Harrison's *Nova Swing*, the anime series *Darker Than Black*, and Jeff VanderMeer's *Southern Reach Trilogy* among others.
6. Meillassoux, 44.
7. Ibid.
8. And Zizek is a case in point, as his recourse to the first *Star Wars* prequel in his *The Fragile Absolute* should demonstrate.

Chapter One

1. This story was originally published in *The Future Fire* in 2016.

Chapter Two

1. Fisher, 2.
2. Dean, 53.
3. This was my argument in *The Communist Necessity*.
4. This is precisely what happened at a Historical Materialist conference at York University in 2007 when Aijaz Ahmad, an ideologue of the CPI(Marxist), delivered a speech where he claimed the future of revolutionary movements was in

peasant and Indigenous rebellions in the peripheries. When he was asked, in the Q&A, to explain how he could make such a claim when his party was actively suppressing a people's war led by peasants, Indigenous Adivasis, and lower caste militants, Ahmad refused to answer and in fact walked off the stage.

5. I discussed this particular issue in my essay "Quartermasters of Stadiums and Cemeteries" in the *Journal of Socialist Studies* (Winter 2016).

6. Really, I think we could write the most contradictory and non-sensical history of the left if we collected all the claims about Stalinism and compiled them into a single document.

7. Fisher, 39–53.

8. In the past decade and a half, however, a number of books dedicated to explaining the New Communist Movement's significance have been written: Max Elbaum's *Revolution in the Air*, Aaron Leonard and Conor Gallagher's *Heavy Radicals*, and Roxanne Dunbar-Ortiz's *Outlaw Woman*.

9. One of Sriduangkaew's skills as an author lies in her characterization of compromised subjects. In most of her fictions she presents characters whose struggles emerge from a combination of the rejection of the fictional state of affairs and the difficulty of transcending socialization. Sometimes these characters are cynical noir individuals, such as the detective of this specific story who struggles with the legacy of her tragic romance with a Himmapan denizen, sometimes they are the powerful agents of *Comet's Call* who are pulled into regional conflicts because of their desires and secrets, and sometimes they are the colonized subjects of *A Universe as Vast as Our Longing* who intentionally accept compromise so as to keep living. The overall point, however, is that socialization produces the grounds for compromise; individuals, especially when they are isolated and separated from broader social movements, cannot be anything but.

Chapter Four

1. Benjamin, 257–258.
2. Ibid., 260.
3. Ibid., 257.
4. Ibid., 260.
5. Ibid., 259.
6. Amin, *Class and Nation*, 1.
7. Ibid.
8. Amin, *Eurocentrism*, 7.
9. Ibid., 8.
10. Fanon, 217–218.
11. Ibid., 218.
12. *Re-Membering the Dismembered* (2005).
13. Fanon, 222.
14. Benjamin, 256.
15. There are many examples of a backwards looking cultural nationalism undermining revolutionary movements, transforming the leaders into imperialist managers of new structures of oppression. One that an author such as Amin would have had in mind when he wrote *Class and Nation* and *Eurocentrism* would be the revolution in Zanzibar, led by Amin's friend Abdulrahman Babu, that was undermined by the Tanzanian cultural nationalism of Julius Nyerere's "African Socialism". As Amrit Wilson's *The Threat of Liberation* (London: Pluto Press, 2013) has thoroughly demonstrated, the CIA used Nyerere to undermine and destroy the mass anti-colonial and anti-capitalist movement mobilized by the Umma Party of Zanzibar.
16. Fanon, 223.
17. If there is an image that best represents the history of settler-colonialism it is the London museum that contains the skulls of Zimbabwe's resistance (http://www. telegraph.co.uk/news/worldnews/africaandindianocean/ zimbabwe/11802355/Britain-confirms-Robert-Mugabes-

claim-a-London-museum-has-Zimbabwean-heroes-skulls.
html).
18. Shipley, 6.
19. Ibid., 7.
20. Ibid., 6–7.
21. Ibid., 316.
22. Ibid., 223–224.
23. Ibid., 224.
24. Amin, *Class and Nation*, 1.
25. PCR-RCP, 5.
26. Marx, 15.

Chapter Five

1. This story is a prequel to the novel *Winterglass* (Apex, 2017).

Chapter Six

1. McClintock, 352.
2. The original source of this claim is never directly cited, and sometimes takes different forms: "wading through rivers of blood" is another common attribution.
3. Benjamin, 260.
4. Ibid.
5. Hegel, *Science of Logic*, 550.
6. Hegel, *Elements of the Philosophy of Right*, §2.
7. Ibid., §15.
8. Ibid.
9. Ibid., §127.
10. Ibid.
11. Ibid.
12. Ibid., §135.
13. Ibid., §44.
14. Ibid., §258.
15. Engels, *Anti-Duhring*, 106. Nature, for Engels, means in this specific context any external force to which humans may be

subjected—even constructed forces such as governments.
16. Ibid., 146.
17. Mao, 183.
18. Engels, *Socialism: Utopian and Scientific*, 73.

Works Cited

Amin, Samir. *Class and Nation*. New York: Monthly Review, 1980.

Amin, Samir. *Eurocentrism (Second Edition)*. New York: Monthly Review, 2009.

Benjamin, Walter. *Illuminations*. New York: Schocken Books, 1968.

Dean, Jodi. *The Communist Horizon*. London: Verso, 2012.

Engels, Friedrich. *Anti-Duhring*. New York: International Publishers, 1987.

Engels, Friedrich. *Socialism: Utopian and Scientific*. New York: International Publishers, 1998.

Fanon, Frantz. *The Wretched of the Earth*. New York: Grove Press, 1963.

Fisher, Mark. *Capitalist Realism: Is There No Alternative?* Winchester: Zero Books, 2009.

Hegel, GWF. *Elements of the Philosophy of Right*. Cambridge: Cambridge University Press, 2014.

Hegel, GWF. *Science of Logic*. Amherst: Humanity Books, 1969.

Mao Zedong. *On Practice and Contradiction*. New York: Verso, 2007.

Marx, Karl. *The 18th Brumaire of Louis Bonaparte*. New York: International Publishers, 1969.

McClintock, Anne. *Imperial Leather*. New York: Routledge, 1995.

Meillassoux, Quentin. *Science Fiction and Extro-Science Fiction*. Minneapolis: Univocal, 2015.

Morera, Esteve. *Gramsci, Materialism, and Philosophy*. London: Routledge, 2014.

PCR-RCP. *How We Intend To Fight*. (http://www.pcr-rcp.ca/old/pdf/pwd/3.pdf)

Shipley, Tyler. *Ottawa and Empire*. Toronto: Between the Lines, 2017.

Acknowledgments

Benjanun Sriduangkaew

My first and foremost thanks to J. Moufawad-Paul, my accomplice and co-author in this strange and, I think, unique book. When he asked if I was interested in doing a collaboration, I was as flattered as I was surprised; this is not the kind of work I usually do, since I am primarily a writer of fiction (and a media/literary critic, though not so much anymore). Working with his area of philosophy was new to me, but I believe all writers of fiction can easily fall into a comfortable rut, and engaging in something entirely new was welcome to me, as well as an opportunity for growth. It makes good on my intent to delve into radical theory. I'd also like to express my appreciation for his partner Vicky, who has contributed no small amount of labour. I'm deeply grateful to the editors of Zer0 for giving life to this strange, beautiful project.

My literary life would not have been possible without the generosity and patience of many friends. Among them I'd like to thank Mike Allen, Cassandra Khaw, Lavie Tidhar, Silvia Moreno-Garcia, Sean Wallace, Jason Sizemore, Troy L. Wiggins, Andrea Johnson, Steve Berman, Miguel Flores, Vajra Chandrasekera, Emily Wagner and Sioban Krzywicki, to name but a few: it is a long list, and sometimes kindness catches me by surprise. Zoe Stavri, Aaminah Khan and Ana Mardoll have inspired and will always inspire me. The courage of Sam Ambreen and Bex Gerber has been a balm in difficult times and I greatly look up to their strength and their empathy.

This book is dedicated to dreamers in the margins, and that includes all of you. Thank you.

J. Moufawad-Paul

This book has to be the most interesting project I've worked on to date since it has brought together two of my long-standing interests: political philosophy and SFF literature. I have always found respite in good SFF novels and stories, most recently those by Benjanun Sriduangkaew, and thus collaborating on this project was thoroughly enjoyable.

Therefore, first and foremost, I must thank Benjanun for being willing to collaborate with me on this project. I have a deep respect for Bee's literary output and it was exciting to not only engage with her work but explore the ways in which she was engaging with mine. *Methods Devour Themselves* was the culmination of a much longer conversation we've had in Twitter's direct messages; despite all the negative aspects of social media this book would not have been possible without a technology that could create a relationship between people separated by vast distance. When we first discussed the possibility of this extended and formalized conversation I worried that it was better in theory than practice but I think I can say with confidence that the final product has closed the theory-practice gap. Her skill as a writer as well as her concern for theoretical detail pushed me to think through problematics I had never coherently considered. I already miss the process of writing this book but I know the conversation will continue. Indeed, even before this book was conceived, I used aspects of one of her stories as an analogical device for another manuscript and thus, when that book is published, echoes of *Methods Devour Themselves* will persist. And I believe that we will continue our informal conversation into the foreseeable future. Maybe some day we'll meet face to face, instead of through the disembodiment of Twitter, though it's definitely not necessary: the relationship is real no matter what.

Secondly, I should thank Jessica Copley and the Revolutionary Time Symposium held at the University of Toronto on March

25th 2017. I used the opportunity of being an invited speaker to present an early draft of my "Debris and Dead Skin" essay because it both fit the symposium's guidelines and gave me an opportunity to receive feedback necessary to develop it into a chapter. The symposium as a whole marked not only that chapter but, because my "Debris and Dead Skin" provoked Bee's *Krungthep is an Onomatopoeia*, the way in which I thought through aspects of the developing conversation.

Next, since this is a book ostensibly concerned with the work of an SFF author, I would be remiss if I did not thank my fellow SFF geek friends. Ryan Toews immediately springs to mind: one of my oldest friends in Toronto who has also shared my appreciation for cutting edge SFF that politically matters. Also notable in this category is Allos Abis—a long time comrade and someone who has been key to my political development—who has pointed out the importance of SFF for people of colour, particularly "QT POC" who are part of the so-called "millennial" generation.

Fourthly, Doug Lain at Zer0 is owed a particular debt of gratitude. Interested in SFF and critical engagements with SFF he encouraged this unorthodox project when I mentioned its possibility. Zer0's intention to pursue the kinds of projects that other presses might dismiss as "too niche" is laudable. I already owed Lain and Zer0 my thanks for taking a chance with *Continuity and Rupture* when other presses thought it was too "mad" (not my word but one used by someone else) to pursue and so I am grateful that they took this book on as well.

Fifthly, I am thankful that George Ciccariello-Maher agreed to endorse this book after reading an early and nearly complete draft. I was reading his excellent *Decolonizing Dialectics* around the time this project was first conceived and wrote a review of that book following my completion of the "Living in Amber" chapter. Although I did not cite his book in that chapter, in retrospect I believe it influenced my analysis. I recall a moment on Twitter, over a year ago, when I joked with George about writing "feisty blurbs" for radical books. I'm very grateful that he did not fulfil his promise to write a blurb composed mainly with emojis.

Finally, no acknowledgments are complete without thanking my life partner, Victoria Moufawad-Paul, for her support and influence. Vicky and I consistently edit each other's work and encourage our respective trajectories. This book in particular is one I know that Vicky really thought worth pursuing since it intersected with many of her concerns in the cultural sphere. It's really great to be in a creative relationship where both partners influence and encourage one another.

Zero Books

CULTURE, SOCIETY & POLITICS

Contemporary culture has eliminated the concept and public figure of the intellectual. A cretinous anti-intellectualism presides, cheer-led by hacks in the pay of multinational corporations who reassure their bored readers that there is no need to rouse themselves from their stupor. Zer0 Books knows that another kind of discourse – intellectual without being academic, popular without being populist – is not only possible: it is already flourishing. Zer0 is convinced that in the unthinking, blandly consensual culture in which we live, critical and engaged theoretical reflection is more important than ever before.

If you have enjoyed this book, why not tell other readers by posting a review on your preferred book site.

Recent bestsellers from Zero Books are:

In the Dust of This Planet
Horror of Philosophy vol. 1
Eugene Thacker
In the first of a series of three books on the Horror of
Philosophy, *In the Dust of This Planet* offers the genre of horror
as a way of thinking about the unthinkable.
Paperback: 978-1-84694-676-9 ebook: 978-1-78099-010-1

Capitalist Realism
Is there no alternative?
Mark Fisher
An analysis of the ways in which capitalism has presented itself
as the only realistic political-economic system.
Paperback: 978-1-84694-317-1 ebook: 978-1-78099-734-6

Rebel Rebel
Chris O'Leary
David Bowie: every single song. Everything you want to know,
everything you didn't know.
Paperback: 978-1-78099-244-0 ebook: 978-1-78099-713-1

Cartographies of the Absolute
Alberto Toscano, Jeff Kinkle
An aesthetics of the economy for the twenty-first century.
Paperback: 978-1-78099-275-4 ebook: 978-1-78279-973-3

Malign Velocities
Accelerationism and Capitalism
Benjamin Noys
Longlisted for the Bread and Roses Prize 2015, *Malign Velocities* argues against the need for speed, tracking acceleration as the symptom of the ongoing crises of capitalism.
Paperback: 978-1-78279-300-7 ebook: 978-1-78279-299-4

Meat Market
Female flesh under Capitalism
Laurie Penny
A feminist dissection of women's bodies as the fleshy fulcrum of capitalist cannibalism, whereby women are both consumers and consumed.
Paperback: 978-1-84694-521-2 ebook: 978-1-84694-782-7

Poor but Sexy
Culture Clashes in Europe East and West
Agata Pyzik
How the East stayed East and the West stayed West.
Paperback: 978-1-78099-394-2 ebook: 978-1-78099-395-9

Romeo and Juliet in Palestine
Teaching Under Occupation
Tom Sperlinger
Life in the West Bank, the nature of pedagogy and the role of a university under occupation.
Paperback: 978-1-78279-637-4 ebook: 978-1-78279-636-7

Sweetening the Pill
or How We Got Hooked on Hormonal Birth Control
Holly Grigg-Spall
Has contraception liberated or oppressed women? *Sweetening the Pill* breaks the silence on the dark side of hormonal contraception.
Paperback: 978-1-78099-607-3 ebook: 978-1-78099-608-0

Why Are We The Good Guys?
Reclaiming Your Mind from the Delusions of Propaganda
David Cromwell
A provocative challenge to the standard ideology that Western power is a benevolent force in the world.
Paperback: 978-1-78099-365-2 ebook: 978-1-78099-366-9

Readers of ebooks can buy or view any of these bestsellers by clicking on the live link in the title. Most titles are published in paperback and as an ebook. Paperbacks are available in traditional bookshops. Both print and ebook formats are available online.

Find more titles and sign up to our readers' newsletter at http://www.johnhuntpublishing.com/culture-and-politics

Follow us on Facebook at https://www.facebook.com/ZeroBooks

and Twitter at https://twitter.com/Zer0Books